"I can't tell you ho[...] you coming over to talk to him," Mallory said, her eyes still misty. *"It's not easy relating to a little boy, especially when handling all the day-to-day stuff is still so new to me."*

"Thanks for calling me," Rick said. "I have to admit, this sort of thing is a little out of my league, but I tried to remember what it was like to be his age."

"Well, your instincts were spot-on. And everything you said to him was perfect." She reached out her hand, although he wasn't sure why.

In appreciation? As a way of extending some sort of parental olive branch?

Or was she hinting that it was time for him to go?

Either way, he took her hand in his. But the moment they touched, a jolt of heat shot right through him.

* * *

RETURN TO BRIGHTON VALLEY:
Who says you can't go home again?

Dear Reader,

I've received a lot of letters from those of you who have enjoyed my stories set in Brighton Valley—The Texas Homecoming, Brighton Valley Medical Center and Brighton Valley Babies—asking me if there will be any more. So here we go again! Welcome to a new series, Return to Brighton Valley. In each of the next three books, one of the characters left town years ago, never wanting to look back. Yet events have brought them home to face the past, which means dealing with the memories and heartache they'd hoped to forget.

In *The Daddy Secret,* Mallory Dickinson was seventeen, unwed and pregnant when she left Brighton Valley. Her plan was to give up her baby for adoption and to return to town, with very few people the wiser. But when given the opportunity, Mallory chose an open adoption and stayed back East so she could be close to her son and to the wonderful couple who adopted him.

Still, a lot can happen in ten years. And when she moved home ten years later, bringing her son with her, the last person in the world she expected to run into was Rick Martinez. Granted, Rick isn't the same hell-bent teenager who'd once stolen her heart and fathered her child, but he's still just as breathtakingly handsome.

When Rick sees that Mallory has finally come back to town, his own battered heart soars—until he sees her son, a nine-year-old boy who resembles him. As you can guess, there are all kinds of sparks flying in this story. So kick back and enjoy another visit to Brighton Valley—and see how Rick and Mallory rekindle their star-crossed first love and make it one that will last forever.

I love hearing from my readers. Feel free to contact me through my website, www.judyduarte.com, and let me know what you thought of this story. I hope you enjoy reading it as much as I enjoyed writing it.

Wishing you all the best.

Happy reading!

Judy

The Daddy Secret

—

Judy Duarte

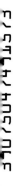

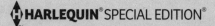
HARLEQUIN®SPECIAL EDITION®

Recycling programs
for this product may
not exist in your area.

ISBN-13: 978-0-373-65800-8

THE DADDY SECRET

Printed in U.S.A.
www.Harlequin.com

JUDY DUARTE

always knew there was a book inside her, but since English was her least favorite subject in school, she never considered herself a writer. An avid reader who enjoys a happy ending, Judy couldn't shake the dream of creating a book of her own.

Her dream became a reality in March 2002, when Silhouette Special Edition released her first book, *Cowboy Courage*. Since then she has published more than twenty novels. Her stories have touched the hearts of readers around the world. And in July 2005 Judy won a prestigious Readers' Choice Award for *The Rich Man's Son*.

Judy makes her home near the beach in Southern California. When she's not cooped up in her writing cave, she's spending time with her somewhat enormous but delightfully close family.

To my mother, Betty Astleford, who was my biggest fan, even before I uttered a single word, let alone formed them into sentences and put them to paper. I love you, Mom!

Chapter One

Mallory Dickinson had vowed years ago that she'd never return to Brighton Valley. But here she was, back in town, listening to the empty moving van pull away from the curb of her newly rented home on a quiet, tree-lined street. One nice thing about the neighborhood was that it wasn't far from the Brighton Valley Medical Center, where her grandfather, a recently retired minister, was hospitalized.

Alice Reilly, who worked part-time at the church, lived across the street. As luck would have it, the kind-hearted woman had been the one to find her grandfather unconscious and to call paramedics. She'd also contacted Mallory and let her know how seriously ill he was. And then, last week, when Alice had learned that the house in her neighborhood was available for rent, she'd called both Mallory and the landlord, setting her cross-country move into motion.

As Mallory studied the small living room, thinking of all the unpacking she had to do, a bark sounded behind her, followed by a couple of bumps, a thump and a swoosh.

She turned to the front door, which apparently the movers had failed to shut tightly when they left, just as a big dog with muddy feet rushed into the house and skidded to a stop in front of her.

"Hey!" she said. "You don't belong in here."

The goofy mutt looked friendly enough, so she reached for its blue collar in an attempt to take it outside before it could track any more mud across the hardwood floor. But she'd no more than skimmed her fingers along the fur on its neck when the mutt jerked to the left, bumping a table with its rump and knocking over her grandmother's antique crystal vase filled with the yellow roses Alice had brought over as a welcome gift an hour earlier.

She winced at the shattered glass, the scattered flowers and the puddle of water on the hardwood floor, as well as the smeared muddy paw prints.

The vase, along with several other valuables and breakables, had been packed in a box marked Priority. She'd opened it immediately upon the van's arrival to make sure the movers hadn't broken any of the contents.

They hadn't, of course. And when Alice had brought the flowers...

But she quickly shut out her reason for setting out something so precious, so valuable, so soon, and shifted her focus to the dog that now headed toward the stairway.

Before she could protest or curse the negligent pet owner who'd let the animal run loose, especially after a spring rain had dumped nearly an inch of water over-night, the critter took off upstairs, its dirty feet undoubt-edly tracking up the new beige carpet.

"No!" she yelled. "Don't go up there. You come back here. *Now!*"

Before she could dash after the darn mutt, a man's voice sounded behind her. "Excuse me, but did a dog just run in here?"

Mallory spun around, ready to give the dog's owner a piece of her mind—and to tell him that he owed her the cost of cleaning the carpet—until her gaze met a familiar face.

Rick Martinez?

Her breath caught, and her jaw must have dropped clear to the floor. She wasn't sure what surprised her more—the fact that the notorious Brighton Valley High School bad boy, a sinfully gorgeous adult version, was standing in her doorway. Or that she still had the same breath-stealing reaction to a pair of dazzling blue eyes she'd never expected to see again.

"Mallory?" he asked, clearly just as astonished to see her.

She had to close her mouth before she could respond, yet even as her lips pressed together, then parted again to allow her to speak, the words only wadded up in her throat.

She finally managed a nod.

He glanced at the broken vase, at the muddy paw prints on the floor. "Oh, no. Did Buddy do that? I'm so sorry. I'll pay for the damages. Where did he go?"

She pointed upstairs.

Rick whistled, then called, "Buddy!"

A bark sounded, and the dog came bounding down

the stairs to its master, its tongue dangling from its mouth.

When it plopped down on its haunches, its muddy tail swooshing across the hardwood floor like a dirty dust mop, Rick slipped his hand under the collar and snapped on the leash. Then he straightened and scanned the cardboard-box-filled room. "Did you just move in?"

At that, she finally found the words to go along with her nod. "Yes."

"That's a surprise."

Wasn't it, though!

She'd loved Rick once, with all her heart. But things had changed.

He'd changed.

She'd changed.

They stood there for a moment, caught up in some kind of weird time warp, where nothing made sense. The air grew thick, making it hard to breathe.

Rick seemed to gather his wits first, as he took another glance at the mess his dog had made. "I'm really sorry about this, Mallory. Buddy has the heart of a puppy and still has a lot to learn. I'm afraid he jumped the fence and was exploring the neighborhood. I'll walk him back to my place, then I'll come back and help you clean up."

His place? Did that mean Rick Martinez was one of her neighbors?

If she'd known that, she never would have agreed to take this house, no matter how cute it was. In fact, she'd assumed that he'd moved away from here years ago, like the teenage drifter he'd claimed to be when she'd first met him, when he'd had to move from his uncle's home to foster care.

Well, apparently her assumption had been wrong.

But there was no way she could accept his offer of help. No way at all.

"You don't need to do that," Mallory said. "I'll take care of it."

"I can't leave you with the mess."

Why couldn't he? She'd cleaned up the mess they'd made of their young lives years ago all on her own, hadn't she?

"So you're back in town," he said again, as if finding it difficult to believe. But then again, why wouldn't he be surprised? After the first few months, she'd never expected to come back, either.

"My grandfather is having some health issues," she said. "I need to be close to him."

Rick nodded as if that all made sense. And while his family hadn't been close, he should understand. Mallory's grandparents had raised her after her parents had died. Gram was gone now, too, and Grandpa was all she had left.

Grandpa and Lucas.

Oh, no. *Lucas.*

Please don't let Alice bring him home now. Not until I've had time to think things through, to decide what to say to who—and when.

Things were complicated. And it would be tough to explain, especially when it was sometimes hard for her to believe how it had all come to be.

"Well," Rick said, "I'd better take Buddy home. But I meant what I said about helping you clean up. I'll also pay for any damages the dog might have caused you. Like the broken vase and the cost of the carpet cleaning."

"Don't give it another thought," Mallory said, eager

to see him go, to begin the cleanup, to put her home and her life back to right again.

As Rick turned and walked his dog outside, Mallory followed him to the porch and waited until he started down the sidewalk. When he finally reached the street, she reentered the house and closed the door. Only then did she breathe a sigh of relief.

Of course, she wasn't foolish enough to think that the relief would last very long. If Rick lived nearby, which he apparently did, eventually they'd run into each other again. And one of these days he'd undoubtedly cross paths with Lucas.

She had no idea what Rick would think, what he'd say, how he'd react when she finally told him about the amazing chain of events that had occurred since she'd left Brighton Valley—if she actually said anything to him about them at all.

She might be older and wiser, but for the second time in ten years, Mallory feared what the future would bring.

It wasn't every day that a guy ran into the girl who'd broken his heart as a teenager, so to say that Rick had been surprised to see that Mallory Dickinson was back in Brighton Valley and living just down the street was a no-brainer.

He'd been sucker punched by the sight of her, by the shoulder-length blond hair that was just as glossy as he remembered, by the big green eyes that had grown even more expressive over the years, by the knockout shape that was far more womanly than when she'd been an innocent teenage girl and he'd been an angry, rebellious teenager on a fast track to nowhere.

Back then, he'd had a chip on his shoulder a mile wide—due in large part to all the times he'd had to change schools. He'd just transferred to Brighton Valley High at the end of his junior year, and he'd been tempted to drop out. But when he met Mallory in the high school cafeteria, he'd been slammed with a classic case of puppy love for a real-life good girl who attended church, even when it wasn't Sunday.

The beautiful college-bound blonde and a full-blown zap of adolescent hormones had done what the teachers, guidance counselors and school psychologist had never been able to do—get him to knuckle down and study. And before he knew it, he was getting his homework done, acing tests and avoiding detention.

He might have complained to his friends about the fact that Mallory had him toeing the line, but he really hadn't minded. For once in his life, someone really cared about him and what his future held.

But then again, things weren't always what they seemed. Whatever he'd felt for Mallory had blown up in his face, leaving him hurt beyond measure and once again shut out by someone he'd thought he loved, someone who'd claimed to have loved him.

Buddy tugged at the leash, and Rick held him steady. "What am I going to do with you, boy? You have to stop jumping the fence and digging out of the yard."

Across the street, coming out of Alice Reilly's house, a dark-haired boy trotted down the porch steps. Rick hadn't noticed him in the neighborhood before. But Alice was always taking in strays of one kind or another—just like Rick did, only hers had two legs instead of four.

"Hey," the boy called out to him. "Nice dog. What's his name?"

"Buddy."

"Can I pet him?"

"Sure." Rick held the dog steady while the boy jogged to the gate, then let himself out of Alice's picket-fenced yard.

Buddy was one of Rick's rescue animals. He'd been brought to the veterinary clinic by a couple of college students who'd found him abandoned by the side of the road and knew he would die without medical help. Buddy, who'd been malnourished, dehydrated and septic from an infected leg wound, was barely alive when the kids had dropped him off.

Rick had told them to leave the dog with him, knowing he'd probably never see any payment. He'd never seen the college kids again, either.

In the meantime, after Buddy responded to the antibiotics and treatment, Rick moved him from the clinic to the rescue yard, planning to find him a new home. But it soon became apparent that the rambunctious Buddy would need some obedience training before he was ready to become a real family pet. Otherwise, whoever adopted him might give up on him and abandon him to a shelter because of his rascally ways.

As the boy ruffled the dog's head, Buddy gave him a sloppy kiss, which caused the kid to laugh. "He likes me."

"I can see that."

"I sure wish I had a dog," the boy said.

"Oh, yeah? Well, it just so happens that Buddy is looking for a home."

"No kidding?" The boy looked up at him with big,

blue eyes, reminding him of one of those trusting expressions Joey, his kid brother, used to flash at him years ago. "You mean Buddy doesn't live with you?"

"He lives with me, but only until I can find him a home with a real family."

"Wow. That would be way cool to have a dog of my own. I always wanted one, but when we lived in the city, my dad said it wouldn't be fair to an animal to keep him cooped up inside all day long. But now I live in a house with a yard."

A squeaky screen door swung open, and Alice Reilly stepped onto her porch. "Oh, there you are, Lucas. I see you've met Dr. Martinez."

The boy, who'd been looking over his shoulder at Alice, turned back to Rick. "You're a *doctor?*"

"Yes. Actually, I'm a veterinarian."

"Cool. Just like Dr. Doolittle, huh? Buddy's lucky to have you."

Rick laughed. "Apparently Buddy isn't so sure about that. He's still trying to decide if there's a better place he'd rather live. Otherwise he'd stay in the yard or on the leash."

"If I can get permission, I'd like to keep him," Lucas said. "We might need a need a bigger, better fence, though."

Rick studied the kid for a moment, noting his short, dark brown hair and the cowlick that grew much like his own. His blue eyes were also a little unusual in those with a darker skin tone. But then again, Rick had Hispanic blood and blue eyes. It happened. He credited his olive complexion to his old man and one of his blue-eyed genes to his Norwegian mother.

Talk about mismatched couples. Rick had given up

trying to figure out why his parents had gotten married in the first place, let alone why they'd stuck together long enough to make everyone around them miserable.

He'd always found genetics interesting, but psychology had never been one of his favorite subjects. Maybe because his family had been so screwed up and it would have given the most gifted therapist a headache to try and figure out a way to straighten them out.

Rick glanced across the street at the house where Mallory had just moved in, then back at Lucas.

No, it couldn't be. Mallory was as honest as the day was long. She wouldn't have deceived him like that and not said a word about it. Besides, the boy—Lucas—had mentioned having a dad and referred to his parents. And Mallory wasn't married. At least, she hadn't been wearing a ring—Rick had checked.

Still, he'd have to find time to talk to her one of these days. There were a few things he'd like to ask her, like why she'd quit taking his calls. And why she hadn't come back to Brighton Valley when she'd said she would.

If they were going to be neighbors, they'd be running into each other on occasion. And it might be best to address some of that stuff and get it out of the way so they could each move on with their lives and not be uncomfortable around each other.

He'd have to stop by her house another time, when he didn't have Buddy to worry about.

He'd told her he'd come back and help clean up Buddy's mess, which would give them an opportunity to talk then. But she'd been pretty adamant about doing it herself. Maybe they both needed to put some time and distance between them until they got used to the idea that they were going to be neighbors.

"Well, I'd better get home," he told Lucas and Alice. "It's feeding time at the zoo."

"You have a *zoo?*" the boy asked, his eyes growing even wider than before.

Rick laughed. "It feels that way sometimes, but no, it's not a real zoo. I do have quite a few rescued pets, though. Maybe Alice will bring you to visit someday."

"Will you, Mrs. Reilly?" Lucas turned to the gray-haired woman, reminding Rick that polite kids didn't call their elders by their first names. Then again, he'd never had lessons in courtesy when he'd been growing up.

"I'd be happy to," Alice told Lucas. "That is, as long as our visit is at a convenient time for Dr. Martinez."

After saying goodbye, Rick took one last glance across the street at Mallory's new digs before taking Buddy home.

All the while, his thoughts drifted to the baby he and Mallory had conceived, the child they'd given up for adoption. He had no idea if the baby had been a boy or a girl, but he thought about it a lot, especially when he spotted a kid about the age their baby would be now.

He hoped that he or she had ended up with better parents and a much better home than Rick and his brother Joey'd had. The fear that he might not have been able to offer the poor kid much better was the only thing that had forced him to sign the papers and lose all ties to his son or daughter.

Well, that and the fact that Mallory and her grandparents hadn't left him with any other options.

* * *

That night, after dinner was over and Lucas had bathed, Mallory took her own shower and slipped into her nightgown. Then she grabbed a book from one of the boxes she'd yet to unpack and went to the living room before going to bed.

She hadn't even read three paragraphs when a knock sounded at the front door.

Who could that be?

A new neighbor, welcoming her to Brighton Valley? It was nearly eight and pretty late for a visit like that. She set aside the novel, got to her feet and headed for the door.

"Yes?" she asked before reaching for the knob.

"Mallory, its Rick Martinez."

At the familiar sound of his voice, her heart nearly leapt out of her chest.

She had no idea how long she stood there, wondering what to say, what to do.

"Are you there?" he asked.

Well, there was no getting around it, she supposed. So she took a deep breath, then slowly blew it out before unlocking the deadbolt and opening the door to see what he wanted.

Tonight, standing under the porch light and wearing a pair of worn denim jeans and a black T-shirt, he didn't appear anywhere near as conservative as he had earlier. In fact, he reminded her of the rebellious teen she'd once known.

His hair was still damp, as though he, too, had just stepped out of the shower.

"I hope it's not too late." His gaze moved from her

eyes, to her lips, to her throat and lower, before making its way back to her face.

She'd been so caught up in the way he filled out his T-shirt, in the realization that he still resembled a rebel, either with or without a cause, that she'd forgotten the fact that she was only wearing a flimsy, lightweight robe over a thin cotton gown.

"I…uh…" She fiddled with the lapel, tugging at it, hoping her nipples didn't show through the soft and comfy but well-worn fabric.

"There are a few things I wanted to talk to you about," he said. "I think it'll make running into each other a little easier from now on."

She folded her arms across her chest. "Yes, I know. And you're probably right. But now really isn't a good time."

"Why?"

There were plenty of reasons. For one thing, she'd been harboring the pain of their breakup for years and had put it behind her. Why stir things up now?

And if that wasn't enough, Lucas was upstairs, although he'd been so quiet that he might have fallen asleep.

But mostly she didn't want to enter any kind of discussion with Rick Martinez while she was dressed in her nightgown, especially since he'd always made her a little uneasy.

He'd also had a way of exciting her, too, and apparently none of that had changed.

Everything else in her life had, though. She'd kicked the dangerous Rick Martinez addiction years ago.

She had a new man in her life now, a stockbroker who cared enough about her to ask his investment firm to transfer him to their Wexler office so they could be together.

Brian Winslow didn't stir her blood the way Rick once had, but they were mature adults. They were also better suited to each other, with common interests and goals—things that made for an enduring relationship.

Rick's gaze swept over her again, sending her already thumping heart topsy-turvy. She tried to ignore the power he still held over her, hoping that once he'd said what he came to say that it would all go away. That *he'd* go away.

But she wasn't dressed for company, and even if she was, did she want to invite him in and make things more awkward between them than she had to?

She'd never expected Rick to stay in Brighton Valley, especially since she'd known how humiliated he'd been when his uncle had been arrested and convicted for assault after beating his aunt unconscious.

She knew, once he'd turned eighteen, Rick had only stuck around because of her. At least, that's what he'd told her back then.

"I...uh... It's not a good time," she said, using the door as a shield, "but if you'd like to come back tomorrow, that would be okay."

He didn't make a move toward leaving, and that same awkward silence stretched before them again.

For a moment, the memories came rolling back, along with the sexual awareness that swarmed around them like lightning bugs in a Mason jar.

What she needed was a diversion.

But the one she got wasn't the one she wanted.

"Hey, Mom," Lucas called from the upstairs landing. "Where did you put my Star Wars Lego set? Is it still in one of the boxes? Or did we forget to bring it when we moved?"

His footsteps sounded as he padded downstairs, and her heart belly flopped into the pit of her stomach. Her whole world was going to blow sky high the moment Rick spotted Lucas.

After all, he'd have to be blind not to see what she saw each time she looked at the boy.

Lucas was the spitting image of Rick Martinez.

Chapter Two

The moment Rick heard Mallory's son call out from the top landing, reality slammed into him like a horse hoof to the chest.

He'd wanted to shove open the door and push past her, but he didn't need to. The boy had enough curiosity for the two of them. Within several pounding heartbeats, he joined his mother at the door.

There stood Lucas, the kid Rick had met earlier, the boy with blue eyes and a cowlick like Rick's.

Of course, Rick might be connecting imaginary genetic dots, but how likely was that?

"Hey! Dr. Martinez. Where's Buddy?"

Rick's first instinct was to launch into an interrogation of Mallory, but he needed to control his gut reaction. Why take out his anger and frustration on the poor kid?

"I'm afraid I left Buddy at home this evening," he said.

Mallory, her eyes wary, her cheeks flushed, looked as if she'd just picked up the wrong end of a hot branding iron. She glanced at Rick, then at the boy. Her *son*. "I didn't realize you two had met."

Apparently not. Would she have mentioned anything about even having a son if the boy hadn't come downstairs?

"We met today," Lucas said. "While I was at Mrs. Reilly's house."

Mallory took a deep breath, then slowly let it out, clearly at a loss and probably trying to buy time in order to gather her thoughts—or maybe to fabricate a lie.

How about that? If there was one thing he could say about Mallory Dickinson, at least the Mallory he'd once known, it was that she was as honest as the day was long.

But it didn't take a brain surgeon to see the writing on the wall. She'd kept the baby she was supposed to have given up for adoption, and she'd let more than nine years go by without telling him.

Betrayal gnawed at his gut, and anger flared in a swirl of ugly colors. He ought to challenge her right here and now, but he couldn't quite bring himself to do it in front of the boy. Apparently, she no longer saw a reason to bar him from entering the house because she stepped away from the door and allowed him in.

"Lucas called you a doctor," she said, arching a delicate brow.

The fact that she found it surprising that Rick had actually made good ought to set him off further, although that was pretty minor in the scheme of things.

Still, he couldn't quite mask his annoyance in his response. "I'm a veterinarian. My clinic is just down the street."

As she mulled that over, Lucas sidled up to Rick wearing a bright-eyed grin. "Did you come to ask my mom about Buddy?"

No, the dog was the last thing he'd come to talk to Mallory about. And while he hadn't been sure just how the conversation was going to unfold when he arrived, it had just taken a sudden and unexpected turn.

"Why would he come to talk to me about his dog?" Mallory asked her son.

Or rather *their* son. Who else could the boy be?

Rick's emotions, which he'd learned to keep in check over the years, spun around like a whirligig, and he was hard pressed to snatch just one on which he could focus.

Lucas, whose smile indicated that he was completely oblivious to the tension building between the adults, approached Mallory. "Because Buddy needs a home. And since we have a yard now, can I have him? *Please?* I promise to take care of him and walk him and everything. You won't have to do anything."

Mallory drew a hand to her chest, just below her throat where her pulse fluttered. "You want a *dog?* I don't know about that."

"Why not?" the boy asked.

She seemed to ponder the question, then said, "We'll have to talk about it later. However, to answer your question about the Legos, I put them on the shelf in the linen closet just outside your bedroom."

"Okay. Thanks." He flashed Rick a smile, then turned and headed toward the stairs.

As Lucas was leaving, Rick's gaze traveled from the boy to Mallory and back again.

Finally, when he and Mallory were alone, Rick folded his arms across his chest, shifted his weight to one hip and gave her a pointed look.

"Cute kid," he said.

Mallory flushed brighter still, and she wiped her palms along her hips, tugging at the fabric of her robe.

Nervous, huh? Rick's internal B.S. detector slipped into overdrive.

Well, she ought to be.

When he'd found out about her pregnancy, he'd only been seventeen, but he'd offered to quit school, get a job and marry her.

However, her grandparents had decided that she was too young and convinced her that giving her child up for adoption was the only way to go. So they'd sent her to Boston to live with her Aunt Carrie until the birth.

Yet in spite of what she'd promised him when she left, she hadn't come back to Brighton Valley. And within six months' time, he'd lost all contact with her. She might blame some of that on him, but he didn't see it that way.

Either way, she'd had a change of heart about the adoption. And about the feelings she'd claimed she'd had for him.

At the thought of Mallory's deception, something rose up inside of him, something dark and ugly and juvenile, something that reminded him that he might always be prone to bad genetics and a lousy upbringing. But he tamped it down, as he'd learned to do in recent years, and glared at the woman he'd once loved instead.

As a teenager, Mallory had attended church regularly. Now she stood warily in the center of her living room looking as guilty as sin.

"Excuse me for being blunt," Rick finally said, "but your son looks a lot like my brother Joey did as a kid."

"It's not what you think."

What he thought was that she'd lied to him, that she'd kept their baby. Was she saying that she hadn't?

"If I'm off base, suppose you set me straight."

She glanced upstairs. "Not here. Not tonight."

Rick wasn't sure if Lucas could hear their conversation or not. But she was right. Any further discussion ought to be done in private.

"All right," he said. "Another time. Preferably tomorrow. You tell me when."

"I…" She bit down on her lip, then glanced upstairs again. "I have a job interview at two o'clock and have already lined up Alice Reilly to babysit. I'll ask her to keep Lucas longer. Would that work for you? We can meet here in the late afternoon."

He had a pretty full schedule at the clinic tomorrow, as well as a couple of minor surgeries. "That's fine, as long as it's after five."

"Okay." She started for the door, signaling that it was time for him to leave.

All right. He'd go for now.

Mallory might have shut him out of her life when they were teenagers, deciding she'd rather raise their son on her own, but a lot of things had happened since she'd been gone. A lot had changed.

When Rick stepped out of the house, she closed the door behind him, shutting him out once again, it seemed.

But he was going to get to the bottom of this once

and for all. He intended to learn more about the baby they'd conceived.

And about the boy who looked like Rick and who called Mallory Mom.

"Excuse me, Dr. Martinez. But there's a lady and a little boy asking to see you. She said her name is Alice Reilly and that you told them to stop by."

Rick, who'd just placed a plastic cone on a German shepherd's head so he couldn't chew at his sutures, glanced up at Kara Dobbins, his receptionist. "They're here? *Now?*"

"Should I tell them to come back another time?"

Rick glanced at his wristwatch. It was 2:25. "Is there anyone in the waiting room?"

"Just Mrs. Reilly and the boy. Tom Randall called and cancelled his two-thirty appointment. He said Duke seems to be doing much better today."

"Tell them I'll be right there. I need to put Samson back in the kennel until the Hendersons come to pick him up."

"I can do that for you," Kara said.

Rick knew he'd told Alice she could bring Lucas to visit the clinic, but he hadn't expected them to show up so soon. Besides, he'd hoped to have that talk with Mallory first. But apparently that wasn't to be. So he'd have to keep his rising suspicion at bay and play things by ear.

When he entered the waiting room, Lucas, who'd been sitting next to Alice, jumped to his feet. "Hi, Dr. Martinez. Thanks for letting us come see your office and all the animals."

"I hope this isn't a bad time," Alice said. "I really

hadn't meant to bring Lucas today, but he was so insistent."

"That's fine," Rick said. "Come with me. I'll show you around."

After a tour of the exam rooms, as well as the hospital boarding area, where Lucas met several of the recovering furry patients, Rick showed him the pharmacy area and the lab. He then let them peer through the glass window into the operating room.

"When I grow up," Lucas said, "I'd like to be a veterinarian, too."

An unexpected sense of pride surged through Rick. Apparently they both shared a love of animals. Did they share anything else?

It's not what you think, Mallory had said.

Oh, no? Then, if Lucas wasn't Rick's son, what had happened to their baby? Had she given it up as she'd said she was going to do? And if so, why did the boy look more like a Martinez than a Dickinson?

According to what Lucas had told Rick yesterday, he had a father. *When we lived in the city, my dad said it wouldn't be fair to an animal to keep him cooped up inside all day long.*

So who had Mallory married? Did he look like Rick? Did he have dark hair and an olive complexion?

Were they still together? Had he moved to Brighton Valley with her?

Rick didn't think so. She hadn't been wearing a ring yesterday. He'd checked again last night. When she'd stood behind the door—hid behind it was more like it—he'd checked out her left hand again. And just as it had been earlier, her ring finger had been bare.

Is that why she'd moved home? For a fresh start?

Probably so. That's why she'd gone to Boston and stayed there, wasn't it? To put Rick behind her?

Alice's voice drew Rick from his musing. "I think you'd make a good veterinarian, Lucas. How good are you in math and science?"

"Pretty good, I guess."

Before Alice could respond, her cell phone rang. She pulled it from her purse and checked the lighted display. "Uh-oh. This is a dear friend whose husband is having some serious health issues. I need to speak to her, Doctor. Would you mind if I left Lucas with you and talked to her in private?"

"No, go ahead."

As Alice stepped through the door that led to the waiting room, Lucas sidled up to Rick. "Where do you keep Buddy?"

"He's in the back, near where I live. Come on. I'll show you." Rick took Lucas out the door that led to the yard enclosed by a chain-link fence.

As they made their way to the gate, Rick said, "I used to let Buddy have the run of the yard, but he kept jumping over the fence."

"He must be a supergood jumper," Lucas said.

"Yes, he is. So I had to lock him in one of the dog runs now, which he doesn't like, but I can't trust him to play in the yard without supervision."

Buddy barked when he spotted them, then wiggled his rump and wagged his tail like crazy. The boy and dog sure seemed to have hit it off. But then, that's the way it was with kids and pets.

But kids and adults?

That wasn't always the case.

Maybe it was best that Rick wasn't the boy's father.

How the hell would he ever relate to him? He hadn't had any kind of role model growing up. Of course, even if the boy was his—and Mallory certainly had implied that he *wasn't*—Rick didn't have to become any kind of SuperDad. Maybe he could just be a friend or a mentor, like Detective Hank Lazaro had been to him.

If Hank hadn't come along when he had and seen something worthwhile in Rick, something that was salvageable and worth tapping into, no telling where Rick would have ended up.

In jail or dead, he supposed.

Either way, that didn't mean Rick wasn't curious about the man who'd replaced him in Mallory's life.

He'd save his big questions for her, but it wouldn't hurt to quiz Lucas a bit—just a few random things that wouldn't seem unusual for a neighbor to ask.

"Hey, Lucas," he said. "I have a question for you. Yesterday, when we were talking in front of Mrs. Reilly's house, you mentioned that your dad wouldn't let you have a dog when you lived in the city."

"Yeah, we had a big brick house but no yard. Now we have a little house and a big yard."

They downsized, huh? "What does your dad do for a living?"

"He was a teacher, but he died when I was seven."

Oops. Rick hadn't seen that coming. "I'm sorry to hear that."

"Yeah, me, too. People said it was a blessing when he died, since he was so sick. But I don't know about that. I mean, why'd he have to get cancer in the first place?"

Rick, who had never been much of a churchgoer except for a couple of times with Mallory when he'd been stuck on her as a teenager, didn't have an answer. And he knew enough not to try and blow heavenly smoke.

No answer had to be better than a wrong one, right?

"I know he's in Heaven now," Lucas added. "And that he has a brand-new body, with hair again and everything. So that's good. But I still wish he was here with me. Know what I mean?"

"Yes, I do."

Rick didn't especially like the idea that Mallory had met another man that she'd fallen in love with, a guy she'd decided would make a much better husband and father than Rick would have made. But apparently the guy had been good to Lucas, so Rick was grateful for that.

And he was truly sorry the kid had had to lose his father, especially since the boy had obviously cared deeply for him.

As Rick opened the latch on the gate, Buddy let out a howl. The minute he was out of the dog run, he rushed out to greet Lucas as though the two were long lost friends.

"You missed me," Lucas said, ruffling the fur on Buddy's neck. "Didn't you, boy."

Buddy gave him a wet, sloppy lick.

As Rick watched the two wrestle and play on the grass, it was hard to guess who was happier—the kid or the dog.

"So, tell me something," Rick said. "What was your dad like?"

"He was just a regular guy, but really nice. Know what I mean?" When Rick nodded, Lucas continued. "He worked at my school and would have been my fourth-grade teacher this year, but he died. So then I had to have Mrs. Callaway instead. And she's cranky and yells all the time."

"I guess it's lucky that you moved to Brighton Valley then. I hear the teachers are much better here." Rick, of course, had heard no such thing, but he wanted to say something to make the kid feel better, although he'd never been very good at stuff like that.

"Dr. Martinez?" Kara called from the doorway to the clinic. "Fred Ames is here with Nugget."

"I'll be right there." Rick strode over to where Buddy was playing with Lucas and grabbed the dog's collar. "I'm afraid I need to go back to work now, so we'll have to put Buddy back into his pen."

"Aw, man. That's too bad. Poor Buddy. I'd hate to live in a cage like that."

So would Rick. In fact, the idea of spending his life in confinement made him think about his uncle, who'd ended up in prison after the last time his drunken rage had turned violent. The neighbors had called the cops, and his aunt had spent a week in the hospital. The state had stepped in, finally, sending Rick and Joey, his younger brother, into foster care.

The whole thing had been pretty embarrassing, since it had been in the local newspaper. Rick had often thought that Mallory's conservative grandfather, a minister, had decided Rick wasn't good enough for Mallory because they figured he would grow up to be like the other men in his family.

To be honest, that was one of the reasons Rick hadn't wanted to settle down, get married and have kids. He'd worried about it a bit, too. Hell, even Joey had run away and cut all ties to everyone who bore a drop of Martinez blood, including Rick.

A couple of years ago, Rick had hired a P.I. and tried to find his kid brother, but it was as if Joey hadn't wanted to be found. He'd pretty much vanished.

Unless, of course, he was dead.

Rick raked a hand through his hair. At times like this, when the memories haunted him, he wondered if he'd really turned his life around or not. Maybe on the outside he had. But on the inside, he feared that he was still the same troubled little boy who'd been knocked around by his old man and called a loser more times than he could count, abandoned by his parents, left to the care of an alcoholic uncle and finally turned over to the state foster system until his eighteenth birthday.

After putting Buddy back in the dog run and locking the gate, Rick and Lucas headed back to the clinic, while Buddy complained with howls and barks.

"I feel bad for him," Lucas said.

So did Rick, which was why he took Buddy for a run each evening and why he let him sleep in the house at night.

Buddy was a free spirit, a lot like Rick. He wasn't cut out to live in a kennel or crate. But if he didn't get his frisky behavior in check, he wouldn't be cut out to be a family pet, either.

Maybe that's why Rick had taken such a liking to the stray, why he'd felt inclined to keep him until he could find a suitable home for him.

Because in some ways, Rick and Buddy were alike. Loners who shouldn't tempt fate.

Mallory's job interview, which had been at the Brighton Valley Medical Center, had gone well, and she suspected the HR director would be calling her for a follow-up interview in the next few days. She had all the qualifications they were looking for in the social worker position, as well as experience at a renowned Boston clinic. In addition to the professional references, she'd also listed a few notable locals, including the former Wexler district attorney, who'd been her grandfather's golfing buddy.

Speaking of Grandpa, she hadn't gotten by to visit him yet today, so she'd have to call him this evening. When she'd told him her plans to adopt Lucas, he'd been a little apprehensive at first, but he seemed to understand. She wasn't sure how much he'd told his friends and associates yet. Alice Reilly knew, so she assumed others did, too.

She still hadn't introduced the two of them. With Grandpa's health what it was, she wasn't sure how taxing that initial visit might be on him. She was also concerned about the effect an awkward meeting would have on her son.

Lucas knew the Dunlops had loved him from the start. They'd chosen him. He'd been their dream-come-true baby.

The adoption, while open, was also child-focused. So Lucas had always known Mallory was his birth mother. But he'd been calling her by her first name ever since he'd learned how to talk, and she'd come to expect it, to appreciate it. Up until his adoptive mother had died, the two of them had a relationship that had been more been more like aunt and nephew.

Just recently, their relationship had begun to change, though, and he'd starting to call her Mom—like he had last night. And she couldn't be happier. But it was all so new, so fragile.

Mallory loved Lucas, and he knew it. But he also knew that she'd given him up to the Dunlops when he was a newborn. She hadn't wanted him to think that she hadn't loved him. Or that she hadn't wanted to be his mother. So she'd let him think that at least part of it had been due to her youth and her obedience to her grandfather's wishes.

Every day she did her best to let him know, one way or another, that she'd never give him up again. That she loved him more than life itself. And he seemed to believe her—thank God, because she meant it from the bottom of her heart.

She was proud of the child he'd become. And she knew her grandfather would be proud of him, too—given the chance. When the two finally met, she wanted everything to be…perfect. And it would be. Soon.

After unlocking the front door, she let herself into the living room. It was nearly five o'clock, and Rick would be coming soon. She wasn't looking forward to their little chat, but he'd been right. The sooner they got it over with, the better.

She left her purse and heels at the stairs, planning to take them to her bedroom later. Then she went to the kitchen, her bare feet padding softly on the cool hardwood floor. She'd no more than poured herself a glass of iced tea when the doorbell rang. That had to be Rick. She took several refreshing swallows, then left the half-full glass on the counter and went to let him in.

As she opened the door, her heart scampered through her chest at the sight of him. He appeared professional again, in a pair of dark slacks and a white button-down shirt. Yet his hair was a bit mussed and rebellious, his eyes wary, his lips still sporting the hint of a scowl.

Would she ever know which Rick she'd meet on any given day?

"Come in," she said, stepping aside so he could enter. "And have a seat."

He slowly sauntered toward the sofa and sat down.

Mallory glanced down at her bare feet, at the pink polish on her toes, but she could feel his eyes on her, angry, hurt.

She didn't like disappointing people, failing them. And while she'd done her best to make up for the one big mistake she'd made ten years ago, here was Rick, stabbing at her guilt and stirring up the old memories, the emotions all over again.

When she looked up, her gaze met his. She saw the accusation in his eyes. *You lied to me.*

He must have read the answer in her own because he shook his head and said, "You told me you were giving our child up so I'd sign those forms and relinquish custody."

"I did give him up."

"But Lucas looks just like me. And he called you Mom."

When he'd recently begun to call her Mom it had warmed her heart to know that their relationship had truly begun to morph into the real deal. But now, she found herself having to explain why something so good, so sweet, wasn't a bad thing.

"I told you that I was going to ask for an open adoption, remember? I even mentioned Sue and Gary Dunlop, the couple who adopted him. She was a nurse, and he was a fourth-grade teacher. They'd been married for nearly fifteen years, and while they'd tried for a long time, they couldn't have kids. You would have loved them, Rick. They were awesome. Sue taught Sunday school at their church, and Gary used to coach Little League and soccer. I couldn't have chosen better people to raise Lucas."

His expression, once hard, seemed to soften a bit, yet doubt still troubled his eyes. "Lucas told me his dad died, but I assumed he meant your husband."

"No, he was talking about Gary." Mallory's eyes filled with tears, just as they always did when she thought of the unfairness of it all, and her voice wobbled when she spoke. "Gary was diagnosed with cancer when Lucas was in first grade. He died a year later."

Rick raked a hand through his hair, mussing it all the more. "And Sue?"

Mallory opened her mouth to speak, but the words didn't form right away. If truth be told, she and Sue had grown really close over the years. Sue had become the big sister Mallory had never had, the mother figure she'd lost as an adolescent. The best friend she might never replace.

"Sue was…" Mallory cleared her throat, hoping the lingering grief would allow her to get the story out. "She died in a car accident last year."

When Rick didn't comment, she went on to explain. "After Gary died, Sue was concerned about what would happen to Lucas if she passed away. Neither she nor Gary had any close family—at least, not any they wanted to raise their son. So she asked me if I'd be his guardian if the unthinkable should happen."

"And so you told her okay."

"Of course. I love Lucas. And I loved Sue and Gary, too. I never really thought anything would happen to either of them, and when it did, I was as crushed as he was. It's been tough on both Lucas and me, but we're making the best of it."

She glanced across the room at Rick, watching him, gauging his reaction. He remained silent for so long, she finally said, "You're not saying anything."

"Yes, I know. It's a lot to think about. And I'm not sure how I feel. Confused and overwhelmed, I guess. But in a way, I feel cheated."

"Why is that? You agreed to give him up."

Those blue eyes struck something deep inside of her, setting her heart on end. "I offered to marry you, Mallory."

"We were kids, Rick. You had no job. No way of supporting us. You were living with another family back then. Remember?"

"I know, but I was willing to do whatever I had to."

Mallory crossed her arms. "And if we'd gotten married when we were teenagers, where would we be now?"

He shrugged. "Who the hell knows?"

She waited a beat, then asked, "So now what?"

He blew out a breath. "In some ways, I have no more to offer Lucas now than I did ten years ago, Mallory. I have no idea how to be a father. My old man used to beat me, that is, when he cared enough to come home. And when he was sober enough to stand up. And then, he took off one day and never came back.

"My uncle was better, at least to me and my brother. But when he drank, he used to abuse my aunt. You know all that. So my family history sucks. Yet now that Lucas is here in Brighton Valley, now that I've met him, I'd like the chance to get to know him. And I want him to know me."

"Fair enough." She got to her feet, deciding to put on

her social worker hat for the time being. After all, she wasn't so sure how to coparent with a guy like Rick, either. Or how he'd fit into her life after all these years. "Why don't we take things slow and easy? We can both let things simmer, then talk more about it later."

He pondered that for a moment. "I suppose that makes sense. I need to sort things out, too. How much time are you suggesting?"

"I'm not sure. Weeks. Maybe months."

"Why so long?"

"Parenting is a big deal. I've never had to do it full-time. And neither have you. Lucas has been through so much recently, and he has a lot to sort through. I'm not sure introducing you to him as his birth father is a good idea right now."

Rick stiffened. "Why not?"

"Well, because…" She took a deep breath, then slowly let it out. "Losing his parents was hard on him. And then there was the move. He left everything that was familiar, so it's all been a big adjustment for him. And for me, too."

"You don't want him to know who I am?"

"Not yet."

"Why?"

"Because… Let's just say it's complicated."

Rick crossed his arms. "How so?"

"I… Well, Gary and Sue were always very honest with him. And when he asked me about his biological father…I… Well, I don't want him to think that I lied to him."

"Why would he think that?"

Mallory shifted in her chair. At the time, when he'd asked about his biological dad, she'd given him the kindest, most logical response she could give a child. But in retrospect, she'd made a mistake. She just wasn't sure how to backpedal at this point without making things worse.

Finally, Rick said, "I hope you didn't tell him that I didn't want to marry you. I wanted to, remember? Of course, I now have to admit that your grandfather was right. I didn't have a dime to my name and probably wouldn't have been a good husband and father, although I would have tried. But for the record, you were the one who was responsible for losing contact. You stopped taking my calls."

"You can't blame me for that. Giving up the baby was the hardest thing I've ever had to do. I told you how badly I wanted an open adoption, and you refused to even consider it. In fact, you were adamant. You said that I could either bring the baby home, or leave it in Boston. But if I left it, not to even bother telling you if it was a boy or a girl."

Rick raked a hand through his hair. "I had a hot temper back then. And I was trying to force your hand. The only reason I didn't want an open adoption with a kid living in Boston, when I was dirt-poor and living in Texas, was because I'd never see him. So fatherhood was an all-or-nothing thing for me. I figured you'd see motherhood that way, too."

"I'm sorry, Rick. I didn't know where you were coming from."

"You could have asked."

Maybe she should have. Clamming up had always been his first line of defense, but she'd been too hurt to care about his feelings.

"You know," he said, "that really sucks, Mal."

What did? The fact that they'd both been too young, immature and ill-prepared to deal with the kind of situation a pregnancy had caused? To be honest, even now, with her education and maturity, she still felt a little out of her league when parenting a boy who'd lost so much in such a few short years.

"I can't believe you'd do that," Rick said.

Apparently, they weren't both on the same page. "Do what?"

"Let Lucas think that I didn't want him."

At that, Mallory leaned forward. "Oh, my gosh, Rick. I'd never tell him something like that. For one thing, that would have crushed him."

Rick settled back into the sofa cushion as if relieved. Then, almost as quickly, he straightened up again. "Then what *did* you tell him?"

"I told him—" Mallory paused for a beat, hating to admit it, then pressed on "—that you died."

Rick's eyes widened in disbelief. "Why in the hell did you tell him *that*?"

She hadn't meant to lie, but she'd thought about it over the years. And she'd realized that something innocent and fragile had died inside her when Rick had signed those adoption papers and told her to do whatever she wanted. Then, when she'd had to choose between staying in Boston to be near Lucas or returning to Brighton Valley and Rick, she'd had to bury whatever memories they'd once had—and any hope of a future together.

"At the time it seemed like the easiest way to explain your absence in our lives. Besides, I wasn't sure what had happened to you. I knew that Joey ran away. And given the rumors I'd heard about the fights you'd been involved in and all the drinking, I'd assumed the same thing had happened to you." She almost mentioned his uncle's trial and conviction, but decided to let that ride for now.

Rick stretched his arm out across the back of her sofa. "Listen, Mallory. I'll admit that I got into a lot of trouble after you left Brighton Valley, but when you didn't come back home like you said you would and wouldn't return my calls, I fell into my old habits. In fact, without you in school, I couldn't see any point in being there, either, so I dropped out before Thanksgiving."

She ought to feel a bit justified at the anger she'd carried for years, yet a surge of sympathy shot through her instead, urging her to rise up from her chair, and sit next to him, under his outstretched arm... To lean her head against his shoulder, to caress his knee, to offer words of compassion....

What was wrong with her?

Ten years had passed since she'd last seen him, and yet she still found herself struggling with those same old urges, those same yearnings, those same... What? Feelings?

No, not those. Not anymore. She was no longer a foolish and gullible teenager blinded by his charm.

"So you dropped out of school, and that's my fault?"

Rick's brow furrowed, and his eye twitched. "Yeah, well, back then, I blamed you."

"You don't now?"

"Not for me dropping out of school. That was my own choice, but I rectified it." Rick placed his hand on the sofa's armrest, then stood. "I'm going to go before we both say things that would be better left unsaid. But just so you know, I'm going to respect your wishes and keep my true identity under wraps for the time being."

"Thank you. I appreciate that."

"But don't take too long figuring out a comfortable way to set him straight."

"I'll do my best." She got to her feet, too. "Thank you for understanding."

They merely stood there for a moment. Then Rick moved a couple paces forward, reached for her hand. He gave it a gentle squeeze with a firm grip, sending a bevy of goose bumps fluttering up her arms. "You've got a week, Mallory."

Then he released her hand, leaving her in the middle of the living room as he headed for the door.

A week? She wasn't sure she was following him. "You mean…?"

As he opened the front door, he turned and glanced over his shoulder. His gaze locked onto hers. "You have one week—seven days—to resurrect me."

"Or what?"

"Or I'll tell Lucas myself."

Chapter Three

The afternoon sunlight spilled onto the antique oak and brass in the back office when Rick finally got a chance to read the morning paper. It wasn't often that he could take a break on a workday, but the clinic schedule had been unusually light for a Wednesday.

In fact, he'd even been tempted to let Kara, his vet tech/receptionist, go home early, but the last time he'd done that, a frantic woman with two sobbing kids had rushed in with a six-month-old Queensland Heeler and a year-old lab mix, both of which had gotten into rat poison. The dogs Rick could handle. But trying to calm and reassure the woman and children who were afraid their pets were dying had damn near been his undoing. Kara was so much better equipped to offer comfort than he was, so for that reason alone, Rick hadn't let her go.

As Fate would have it, nothing unexpected had come

up this afternoon. At least, not until Kara approached his open office door.

"Dr. Martinez?"

Rick looked up from the article he'd been reading. "Yes, Kara?"

"That little boy is back. You know, the cute little guy who kind of looks like you?"

She had to be talking about Lucas. And the fact that she'd picked up on their resemblance probably required a response, but Rick wasn't sure what to say, so he let it slide. "Is he with Alice Reilly?"

"No, he's alone. He rode his bicycle and left it outside. He asked if I thought it would be safe out there. He's afraid someone might steal it."

"That's because he used to live in a big city." Rick set the paper aside and stood. Then he made his way to the front of the office, where the boy stood near the fish tank.

When Lucas heard the adults approach, he turned and blessed Rick with a bright-eyed smile. "Hey, Dr. Martinez. I was just checking out the neighborhood and stopped to say hi."

Kara, who'd followed Rick and was leaning against the doorjamb, looked first at Lucas, then at Rick, and back to the boy. She smiled before returning to her desk and whispered, "Amazing."

Rick was definitely going to have to address the issue of his resemblance to Lucas with Kara one of these days, but not now. Not in front of the boy. And not until the week was up and he and Mallory had settled things.

"I also wanted to tell you my good idea," Lucas said.

"Oh, yeah? What's that?"

"When it's summer, and lots of kids get jobs, I

thought it would be cool if I worked for you. And I know just the thing I could do."

Rick couldn't help but smile at his spunk, but hiring him was out of the question. Even if there weren't state laws about child labor Rick had to comply with, the clinic could get busy at times. And he couldn't have a nine-year-old boy underfoot. "I'm afraid I don't need any office help right now."

"I wasn't talking about working in the office," Lucas said. "You could hire me to play with Buddy every day. That way, I could make sure he wouldn't jump out of the fence, and you wouldn't have to keep him locked in the small cage. What do you think?"

The idea was pretty wild, but Rick had to give the kid credit for ingenuity. He'd figured out a way to spend time with Buddy every day once summer rolled around.

"Actually," Lucas said, "you wouldn't even have to pay me, but if it was a real job, my mom would probably let me do it."

So, he was cunning, too. He'd figured out how to get his mother's approval at the same time.

Mallory was going to have her hands full with him when he became a teenager. He was already trying to outsmart her.

"So what do you say?" the boy asked.

"Let me think about it, okay?" Rick would have to talk it over with Mallory, who might not think it was a very good idea—with or without a wage being attached.

"Would it be okay if I played with Buddy now?" Lucas asked. "You wouldn't have to pay me. I'd do it for free."

Did Mallory realize how badly the boy wanted a pet? Probably not. Should Rick go to bat for him?

Just how involved did he want to get?

He hadn't decided yet, but since there wasn't anything going on this afternoon, he didn't suppose it would hurt to let him spend some time with the dog.

"Sure," Rick said. "Let's go play with Buddy."

Twenty minutes later, while Buddy chased Lucas around the fenced yard in back, Rick fed and cared for the other rescue animals—three cats, a rabbit, a Nubian goat and a dun gelding. Yet he couldn't keep from watching his son. It was heartwarming to see Lucas so happy, so carefree.

Too bad Mallory couldn't see him and Buddy together. Maybe she'd consider giving the dog a home. Of course, she and Buddy hadn't gotten off on the right foot—or rather paw. And there'd definitely be a need for some obedience classes.

"Dr. Martinez?" Kara called from the back door of the clinic. "It's nearly five, so I'm going to start locking up."

"Thank you, Kara. Have a good weekend."

"You, too."

Rick turned his attention back to Lucas. It was still hard to wrap his mind around the fact that he and Mallory had conceived a child, but this particular boy, with his ingenuity, his heart for animals and all the other things Rick had yet to uncover about him, intrigued him.

To quote Kara, it *was* truly amazing.

When Lucas ran up, with Buddy on his heels, he had to stop and catch his breath before he could speak. "Did you think about it yet? Would it be okay if I came and played with Buddy?"

"We'll have to talk to your mom about that," Rick said.

"I don't think she'll care, especially when Brian gets here."

"Brian?"

"Her boyfriend."

Rick had made a lot of assumptions about Mallory, all because she'd never told him much about where she'd been and what she'd done after she'd left Brighton Valley. But never once had she hinted at the fact that she had a man in her life. Not that the information was pertinent to their son, but...

Well, for some crazy reason, it felt pertinent to Rick.

"Where does Brian live?" he asked.

"In Boston. But he's going to move to Brighton Valley."

That was a pretty big move for a couple who were just dating. The relationship sounded serious.

"Do you like Brian?" Rick asked.

"He's okay, but he's kind of a nerd. Know what I mean?"

"Why do you say that?"

"Because he doesn't like sports or anything fun. He's not like my dad." Lucas paused, then glanced down at his feet. When he looked up, he swiped at his watery eyes with the back of his hand.

Aw, man. Rick didn't know what to say, what to do.

"My mom died, too," Lucas added. "And sometimes it's really hard. Mallory tries, but she's not..." He stopped, bit down on his lip. "Well, she is, but... It's hard to explain."

"Listen, Lucas. Mallory told me about Sue and Gary Dunlop. And they were your *real* parents. Don't ever forget that. They loved you and chose to be your mom and dad. They stepped in when your birth parents weren't able to."

Rick could have said something then about being his birth father and could have used the opportunity to explain, but he'd promised Mallory he'd wait, and he'd honor that.

He knew he wasn't very good at this sort of thing, but for some reason, he wanted to go to bat for Mallory. And he figured he could do that by saying what he imagined she'd say if she were here with them.

"Mallory loves you, too, Lucas. More than you'll ever know. And the hardest thing she ever had to do was to give you up when she did. But she chose the very best parents in the world for you. And I think she did an excellent job, don't you?"

Lucas sniffled and nodded.

"Mallory is able to be your mom now. And she'll be there for you always. I know it's not the same as it used to be, but in time, I think you'll see that your life will be just as good as it was—only in a different way."

"That's what Mallory said." Lucas sniffled again. "And I love her, too. It's just that…well, you know."

"Yeah, I do know." And while Rick really didn't, not exactly, he had a pretty good idea.

He also did know something else. Mallory had been right. Lucas had been through a lot recently. And while it might not be fair to dump too much of the past on him right now—like a living, breathing birth father— maybe it wasn't fair to throw a potential stepfather at him, either.

The two of them sat like that for a while, lost in their thoughts, lost in their memories and what-ifs.

Rick wished he could tell Lucas who he really was

and that he'd be there for him, too. Maybe not as a real dad or as Mallory's husband, but he could be a substitute for Gary Dunlop.

In fact, the more he thought about being a substitute, the more he liked it.

That way, there wouldn't be the same expectations. And if he screwed up, maybe it wouldn't matter so much.

Rick had no idea where the time had gone, but at a quarter to six, Lucas suddenly realized he was in "big trouble" and had to hurry home. Apparently, Mallory had only given Lucas permission to ride his bike for a few minutes—and to stay "close to the house."

For some reason, Rick felt a little guilty, too, although he wasn't sure why.

As a kid, he'd never had any kind of curfew. He'd just gone home whenever he'd felt like it. In fact, sometimes it had been in his best interest to arrive after his old man—and later, his uncle—had gone to bed.

But he could certainly understand why Lucas wouldn't want to get into trouble. When Rick and Mallory had been dating, he'd wanted her to see his good side, too. And he'd never wanted to disappoint her.

If he knew her phone number he'd call. He could probably get it from Lucas, but her house was just a few blocks away. So thinking that it might help Lucas if he put in a good word in for him, Rick placed the boy's bike in the back of his pickup, then drove him home.

They'd no more than parked along the curb in front of Mallory's house when she rushed out onto the porch to meet them. She was wearing a pair of black slacks, a green blouse and a frantic expression.

"Where have you been?" she asked Lucas. "I've been worried sick and looking all over for you."

"I'm sorry. I went to see Dr. Martinez at the clinic, and we just… Well, I didn't know how late it was."

Mallory, her hands splayed on her hips, shot an angry glare at Rick. "Why didn't you call and let me know where he was?"

Rick's first impulse was to blame Lucas for not mentioning that he had to be home at a certain time, but why throw the boy under the bus?

Besides, a defensive retort like that was only going to make things worse, especially when Rick was in way over his head when it came to parenting. If truth be told, he didn't have a clue what Mallory expected of him as a father, but he couldn't admit that. Revealing his flaws and insecurities so early in the game probably wasn't a good idea.

Instead, he gave the only excuse he could think of. "I didn't have your phone number."

"But you have a watch, Rick. How long was he with you?"

"About two hours, I guess."

"Didn't you realize I'd be looking for him after all that time? Besides, it's getting dark."

"Mallory," Lucas said, "please don't be mad at Dr. Martinez. It wasn't his fault. It was mine."

The boy had called her Mom earlier, but apparently, in the heat of the moment, he'd slipped back to old habits. Or had he done that on purpose as an act of rebellion?

Rick stole a glance at Mallory, saw her softening expression melt into a wounded frown that touched something deep inside of him. And while he was glad that

Lucas had stuck up for him, he hadn't wanted it to be at Mallory's expense.

"I'm sorry," Rick said. "Lucas stopped to see me at the clinic, and while he played with Buddy, I got busy feeding my rescue animals. I should have sent him home earlier, but I didn't. It won't happen again."

Their gazes locked, and the conversation stalled for a moment, then Mallory said, "I'm sorry, too, Rick. I didn't mean to sound so harsh. I was just worried. He's always home before it gets dark."

She tucked a strand of hair behind her ear, looking more vulnerable than he'd ever seen her. More beautiful, too.

The years had been good to her, and if the two of them hadn't shared a painful past, if they'd met for the first time in downtown Brighton Valley, maybe at Caroline's Diner, Rick might have asked her out.

As it was, there was too much water under the bridge for them to consider something like that—no matter how attractive he still found her.

"I promise never to be late again," Lucas said.

Mallory turned to the boy, then wrapped him in her arms and drew him close. "I love you so much, sweetheart. I don't know what I'd do if something happened to you."

"I love you, too."

Rick shoved his hands in his pockets, feeling like the odd man out. But why shouldn't he feel that way? Mallory had placed him in that position a long time ago.

"I'd better go," he said. "It's probably past your dinnertime, and I won't keep you from it any longer."

Mallory released Lucas from her embrace, but kept her hands on his shoulders. "Actually, dinner will be ready in about fifteen minutes. We're having spaghetti tonight, and I have plenty. Why don't you stay and eat with us?"

As hungry as he was, and as tempted as he was to join them, he probably ought to decline. After all, she was just trying to make it up to him for jumping all over him for something that hadn't been his fault.

"Please?" Lucas said. "She makes really good spaghetti."

There were probably a hundred reasons why Rick ought to climb into his truck and go home. But instead of grabbing hold of one of them and running with it, he found himself saying, "Sure. Why not?"

Mallory hadn't meant to snap at Rick for not sending Lucas home or for not letting her know where he was. After all, Lucas knew the rules. He also should have realized that it was getting dark and Mallory would have been worried about him.

So she'd offered the dinner invitation to Rick as a peace offering. Still, she really hadn't expected him to accept. Things had ended badly between them when she'd left town to have their baby, and then again yesterday, when he'd found about Lucas. So the evening was sure to be awkward at best.

She left Rick and Lucas in the living room while she finished in the kitchen, but it didn't take her very long. As soon as the pasta was done, she called them to the table, where they all took their seats, just like a typical all-American family, when they were anything but.

"Mallory, I mean my mom, is a good cook," Lucas said.

Rick looked up from his plate of spaghetti and smiled

at the boy. "She certainly is." Then he looked at Mallory. "The sauce is really tasty. Is it homemade?"

"Yes, it's Sue's recipe. I have her cookbook and have been making all her family favorites."

"We should have Dr. Martinez come over for the tamale pie casserole tomorrow," Lucas said.

Something told Mallory things could really get out of hand if she didn't do something to discourage her son's budding friendship with Rick. But then again, what would happen when she told the boy that the vet down the street was actually his biological father, the man she'd told him was dead?

Gary and Sue had been great parents—close to perfect, in fact. So Mallory had some big shoes to fill. They'd valued honesty above all else and had done their best to teach Lucas to be truthful.

Mallory valued honesty, too! It's just that she'd had a good reason for telling Lucas what she did, when she did.

At the time Lucas had asked about his biological father, Gary had just lost a grueling battle to cancer. She'd feared that Lucas only wanted to find Rick as a means of filling the painful hole his father's death had left in his life.

But how could anyone ever replace a man like Gary Dunlop?

Then there was the fact that Rick might not have wanted to be found. And even if he had, what if he hadn't been able to hold a candle to Gary's memory? What if he would have disappointed Lucas when the poor child had been so vulnerable?

There'd been so many what-ifs, all of which would have hurt the grieving child in the long run. So Mallory had made it simple on them all. She'd told Lucas that she and Rick might have been able to keep Lucas and create a family together if Rick hadn't died. But at her age, raising a child alone wouldn't have been fair to him.

Telling him the truth now might seem like a simple solution to Rick. But it wasn't. Not when Lucas was still learning to put his faith in Mallory as his mother. Besides, how did she explain her reason for lying to him when Rick *hadn't* grown up to be the loser everyone in town had expected him to become?

"Thanks," Rick said, "but I'll have to pass on dinner tomorrow night. I have to attend a meeting at the chamber of commerce. Maybe another time."

Thank goodness that seemed to appease the boy. All Mallory needed was to give Rick a standing invitation to dinner each night. This evening was going to be tough enough.

Fortunately, Lucas kept the conversation going, which was a relief. Mallory had no idea what to say to the man, especially when the only thing she could think about was how darn good the years had been to him, how he'd filled out so nicely.

He might have grown up and shed his bad-boy reputation, but he still had those amazing blue eyes, that crooked grin and that sexy James Dean swagger that spiked her heart rate and sent her hormones racing.

After they'd eaten, Mallory served chocolate ice cream for dessert. If Rick thought she'd chosen the flavor because she'd remembered it was his favorite, he was wrong. It just so happened to be Lucas's dessert of choice, too—another of the many things the two had in common.

"Hey, Mom," Lucas said. "Did you find my Play-Station yet?"

She couldn't believe she'd packed something as important as that without noting which box it was in. Something told her Sue would have known to label it as a high priority, rather than antique vases, crystal and other breakables. But she wouldn't beat herself up for the mistake. She still had a lot to learn about maternal priorities.

"I'm sure I'll find the box soon," she said. "I know we brought it with us."

"You don't think the movers stole it, do you?"

"Of course not," she said. "I'm sure it'll turn up. I'll make a point of finding it first thing in the morning."

Lucas turned to Rick. "Do you like to play video games?"

"When I was your age I used to, but I don't have much time for it anymore."

"I guess that's because, when people grow up, they don't like to play fun things anymore."

"That's not always true," Rick said. "I have a friend who's a computer whiz and a part-time gamer. He's into all that stuff."

"No kidding?" the boy asked, his eyes wide.

Rick looked at Mallory. "Do you remember Clay Jenkins?"

"That nerdy guy with shaggy hair and glasses?"

Rick nodded. "He might have looked like a wimp, but he had a mean left hook, which came in handy whenever he couldn't outthink a bigger guy who wanted to mess with him."

"Clay was that smart?"

"He was a *genius*."

"Whatever happened to him?" she asked.

"He turned a little computer repair shop into a computer franchise called Zorba the Geek."

"I've heard of it. We had one in Boston, not far from where I lived."

"Yeah, well he's worth a fortune now."

Amazing. Clay used to hang out in Wexler Park with that crowd Mallory had asked Rick to stay away from.

"I guess a lot can change in ten years," she said.

Rick merely looked at her with that same simple gaze that set her heart thumping and her pulse dancing, just as it always used to do.

Apparently, some things might change, while others never did.

"Maybe I could meet your friend someday," Lucas said.

"You never know. Clay moved out of state, but he travels a lot. Maybe he'll pass through this way someday. I'll have to give him a call. It's been a while since we talked, and it's time we touched base."

They continued to eat their ice cream. When they finished, Rick offered to help with the dishes.

The last thing Mallory needed was to have him stick around any longer than he already had. With the past hurt and disappointment they both harbored, it was awkward enough. And somehow, she doubted they'd ever be able to put that completely behind them. But what made things worse was that she still found him attractive, and that was a complication she didn't need.

With the job search, concern over her grandfather's slow recovery and trying her best to fill Sue Dunlop's shoes and be the best mother she could be, Mallory didn't have time to deal with rebellious hormones.

"Thanks, Rick. But I don't need any help. I always clean the kitchen as I go, so doing the dishes is a snap."

"Okay, then. If you're sure…"

When he pushed back his chair and stood, she followed him to the door.

"Thanks for dinner," he said. "You're a good cook, Mallory. You're also a good mom."

She'd expected the compliment about the meal. After all, it was the kind of thing dinner guests usually offered their hosts upon leaving. But the other one took her aback, especially since she'd been trying so hard to be a good mother and she wasn't always sure if she was succeeding.

"Thank you," she said. "I'm trying."

They stood on the stoop for a moment, under the amber glow of the porch light. Yet for some reason, she wasn't nearly as eager to see him leave as she'd been earlier.

Why was that?

For the past ten years—at least, for the bulk of them—she'd tried so hard to forget all about him, to pretend he no longer meant the world to her. She'd even gone so far as to tell Lucas that he'd died.

It had helped, she supposed, to pretend that he had. She'd healed from the heartbreak and had gone on with her life, becoming successful and making her family proud once again.

And then, here he was—alive and well, successful in his own right and threatening to stir up all the old memories, all the things she'd tried so hard to forget.

"You mentioned your grandfather was in the hospital," he said. "How's he doing?"

"He's doing better now. He had quadruple bypass

surgery a couple weeks ago, but he has some other health issues, including diabetes, that have complicated things and slowed his recovery process."

"I take it he knows about the adoption."

"Yes, he does." Like Rick, her grandfather hadn't been in favor of an open adoption. So, for that reason, he and Lucas hadn't met before.

He understood why she was adopting Lucas now and approved of the decision. But she hadn't had time to set up an official meeting. She planned to do that soon, though.

That, too, was going to be a little awkward. She wasn't sure how many of his friends knew that she'd had a child out of wedlock and had given it up for adoption, so she and her grandfather would have some explaining to do. She couldn't foresee any problems, though. People in the church were understanding and forgiving. At least, they were supposed to be.

She thought it would help if she could tell her grandfather that Rick had turned his life around, that he'd become a respected member of the community—that is, if Grandpa didn't already know that.

Being able to share that information would certainly help her by lessening some of the tension that was sure to crop up when she had to bring up the topic of her past mistake and her grandfather's subsequent embarrassment. After all, he'd been a minister, and he'd expected her to set an example with the other teenagers in the congregation.

"I've been curious," she said. "How did you come to study veterinary medicine in college? And how did you end up opening a clinic in Brighton Valley?"

"Remember how I used to hang out at Wexler Park?"

How could she forget? She'd encouraged him to do more productive things with his time, and while they'd dated, he had. But she'd heard that he'd slipped back to his old habits after she'd left town.

"One night in December, after you had the baby, my friends and I were playing basketball in the park. We were being pretty loud, and an off duty police officer named Hank Lazaro showed up. I figured we were in trouble since it was so late, but Hank started shooting hoops with us. He was actually pretty good—and kind of cool. When the game was over, he asked if we'd help him serve lunch at the neighborhood soup kitchen the next day."

"No kidding?" That didn't seem like the kind of thing those guys would have wanted to do. "What did you tell him?"

"The next day was Christmas Eve, and we didn't have anything better to do, so we agreed. And when we'd not only fed the homeless but eaten our fill, too, Hank asked if we had plans for that night."

"Did you?"

"At the time, I was living in a buddy's RV, which was parked at a storage lot and didn't have any power. So no, I didn't have any plans. And neither did Clay. So Hank took us home with him. We hung out with him for a while, watching television and shooting the breeze. Then, when it was time for dinner, boy, were we in for a treat. It was a real Normal Rockwell experience—roast turkey, stuffing, mashed potatoes and gravy, pumpkin pie. Clay and I never did figure out how Hank and his wife had managed to put presents with our names on the tags under their Christmas tree."

"The Lazaros sound like nice people."

"They're the best. Hank has an eye for kids who are on the verge of making a life-changing choice—the bad kind. Fortunately for me, he saw something good in me and took me under his wing. His mentoring gradually changed my attitude about the future. He encouraged me to take the GED, and I passed."

"So how did you decide to go on to college and major in veterinary medicine?"

"Hank helped me get a job with Doc Grimes, and I really enjoyed working with sick and injured animals. I decided to become a vet, just like Doc. When I graduated, I went back to work with him. He retired last year, and sold me his practice. Lucas probably told you the rest."

"The rest?"

"I run a rescue for abused and neglected animals in the back."

"Actually, Lucas only talked to me about Buddy and how he'd like to keep him. Is he one of the rescue dogs?"

"Yes, and he really needs a home."

She laughed. "I think what he really needs is some obedience training."

"You got that right."

Neither of them made a move toward saying goodnight, and while she could have, she studied him in the porch light instead.

Was he married?

Probably not. He wasn't wearing a ring. She'd looked. But was he dating or spoken for?

The subject hadn't come up, and there'd been no reason to talk about it. She supposed she could ask—but there was no way she'd do that. He might think she was interested in him, and she certainly wasn't.

She was involved with someone herself—Brian Winslow, who loved her enough to make a big cross-country move to be near her. And thanks to what Lucas had told him a few weeks back, Brian also thought Rick was dead.

Her stomach clenched, and her conscience turned inside out. Why hadn't she corrected that comment, especially when she wasn't entirely sure what had happened to Rick? She'd meant to. And she *would* correct it. She certainly couldn't let Brian continue to think that now.

Especially when Rick Martinez was very much alive and living just down the street in Brighton Valley.

Chapter Four

Rick's clinic with his apartment in back was only a few blocks from Mallory's house, not far enough for him to give their evening together too much thought on the short drive home. But after parking his truck and unlocking his front door, he had a lot more time to ponder all that had gone on—and the changes that Mallory's move back to Brighton Valley would bring.

Over the years, plenty of women had invited Rick over and cooked dinner for him. Most of them had turned on some romantic music and set the table with flickering candles, determined to set the mood for the night to come.

But he'd never had one invite him to stay for a family-style meal. Of course, he'd made it a point never to date women who had children—or anyone who wanted more from him than an exclusive sexual relationship that would last as long as it remained mutually beneficial.

As awkward as dinner at Mallory's house had been at first, he had to admit that it had turned out okay.

Like he'd told her, she was a good cook and a good mother. She'd also created a nice home for Lucas, certainly warmer and more loving than the ones in which Rick and his kid brother had grown up.

At one time, when he'd loved Mallory, he'd actually believed that he stood a chance to finally have the kind of family he'd always wanted, although that hadn't panned out. Once in a while, he still found himself wishing that, someday, somehow, he might be able to shake his past and create a decent home in which he could raise a family of his own. That same hope had once again crossed his mind this evening, especially whenever he'd glanced at Lucas.

Could he set up a place where the boy would like to visit—not just a veterinary clinic with a menagerie of rescued animals, but an actual house with a TV and video games and the other things real families used to turn four walls into a home?

Maybe.

But each time he thought of a home like that, Mallory's image would drift into the picture, and he'd have to blink it all away.

What in the hell was wrong with him?

She had a boyfriend, a guy who was going to move to Brighton Valley one day soon. A man who probably had money, a decent career and undoubtedly the class and social standing to match.

Rick might have a respectable profession, but he still had a few financial concerns, thanks to one last student loan and the payments he made to Doc Grimes on the practice he'd purchased. But social connections and class? With Rick's past, that was probably going to be an uphill battle until the day he died.

After parking his truck, he checked on the animals, then let Buddy out of the pen and took him into the house.

"Are you up for some television before we turn in for the night?" he asked the dog.

Buddy barked, then took off to make a quick scan and sniff of the apartment, apparently checking to make sure everything was just as he'd left it this morning.

Rick stopped by the answering machine, a relic left over from the days when Doc Grimes lived here. Since most people called him at the office or on his cell, he probably ought to eliminate that line altogether. But tonight, a blinking red light indicated he had a message.

He pushed the play button and listened.

"Hi, Rick. It's *Tia* Rosa. I wondered if you'd like to come over for dinner on Saturday. If you're busy, I understand. But either way, I'd like to talk to you." She paused a moment before adding, "Your uncle has been calling me, hoping to get together for coffee or something. And I was… Well, I wanted to ask what you thought about that. I know you've been against it in the past, but this time I think he's really changed. And I'd like to give him a chance. Anyway, call me when you can. You have my number."

Rick blew out a sigh, then deleted the message. He'd return her call, but wasn't looking forward to it. His aunt and uncle were a toxic combination, especially when they drank, so his advice to her wasn't going to change.

His aunt had joined Alcoholics Anonymous after his uncle's conviction for assault, and she'd started working on her other issues, the ones that had led to her drinking in the first place. She'd gotten some counseling through a program for victims of domestic violence and had come a long way, especially in the past few years. He really hated to see her backslide, which he feared would happen if his uncle came back into the picture.

And then where would that lead?

To be honest, Rick was still embarrassed by the whole mess—and not just the assault that had landed his uncle in jail, his aunt in the hospital and he and his brother in foster care. It was the whole five years he'd spent living in their household, moving from town to town and school to school.

He was still trying to shake the memories and to live down the embarrassment, the late night fights, the neighbors' complaints....

And all because of his uncle's drinking, his anger issues and his inability to keep a job.

Up until the time Rick was at Texas A & M, he'd avoided his aunt completely, although he hadn't run away from home, like Joey had. But after a while, he'd realized that it hadn't been Rosa's fault. She'd been as much a victim as he and Joey had been. And when he finally went to visit her at the hair salon in Wexler, where she worked, he realized that she'd changed, just as he was trying to do. So he'd reconnected with her and had kept in contact, although he couldn't say that they were especially close. He still had trust issues and kept her at arm's distance.

He'd visit her at her condominium in Wexler, but he was reluctant to bring her into the new life he'd created for himself. He'd worked too hard to shake the past, and he didn't want to remind anyone in Brighton Valley of the way things used to be when he was a teenager.

After fixing himself a glass of iced tea, he dialed her number. She picked up on the third ring.

"Hi, *Tia.* It's Rick."

"Thanks for calling me back. I see you got my message."

"So Ramon called you again?"

"He's been calling, and it sounds as if he's really made a change in his life this time."

Rick knew how the cycle of violence worked. The abuser would be very sorry and make all kinds of pleas and promises, only to fall back into the same pattern as before. "I've told you how I feel about that, especially if he's still drinking."

"He was sober all the while he was locked up, but there was that time after he got out that he went a little crazy. But he's in AA now. And it's been almost a year."

That probably sounded like a long time to Ramon, but Rick was skeptical, especially for a guy who had a problem as bad as his uncle's.

"Ramon also took anger management classes while in prison," his aunt said. "He swears that he loves me and always has. He wants to reconcile, but I'm not so sure about that."

"You're wise to doubt him."

"I know. But Ramon suggested that we just go out on a date. And I thought it might be nice to…you know, have dinner with him. I get kind of lonely these days. And I did love him once. When he's not drinking, he's a wonderful man. I could probably love him again."

"I don't think that's a good idea," Rick said.

Rosa didn't answer right away. Finally she said, "I had a feeling you'd say that."

"I lived with you back in the day. I remember the fights, the mean things he'd say to you. And don't forget. The alcohol brought out the worst in you, too."

"You're right. But if he's changed…"

"And if he hasn't? Or if he can't help himself from stopping by Finnegan's Pub for just one drink on the way home someday?"

"I know. You're right. It's just that…I really want to believe that he's changed."

"Then maybe you should wait until he's made it the full year."

"I suppose I could do that. I knew there was a good reason to call you." She paused for a moment, then added, "What about dinner on Saturday?"

"Actually, I already have plans. The Lazaros have invited me over for a barbecue."

"All right. Maybe another time."

They made small talk for a while, then ended the call.

As Rick hung up the receiver, he blew out a sigh. What were the chances that Uncle Ramon had really gone on the wagon for good? Or that he'd managed to control his anger?

All Rick needed was for a new family drama to draw him back into the past, especially now that Mallory had returned to town. He'd finally created a respectable life for himself. And he had a purpose, one that suited him.

What more could he ask for?

While finding his brother and having a family of his own would be nice, he'd pretty much given up on both.

Rick had learned early on that some dreams would always be just beyond his reach.

* * *

By the time office hours rolled around the next day, Rick had decided to steer clear of Mallory and Lucas for a while. He might have given Mallory a week to tell Lucas the truth about his biological father—and who he really was—but he was no longer sure he should push her on the deadline. She wasn't the only one who needed time to reconcile the past with the present and to figure out how it was going to play out in the future.

Sure, he had every intention of having a relationship of some kind with his son, but the last thing he wanted or needed was to get emotionally drawn into a situation that was out of his comfort zone.

Yet even though he'd decided to put some distance between him, Lucas and Mallory, apparently Lucas had other plans.

"Dr. Martinez?" his receptionist called out from the doorway of his small office in the back of the clinic.

Rick glanced up from the paperwork on his desk. "Yes, Kara?"

"Lucas is out in the waiting room and wants to talk to you when you have a few minutes."

Again? What was Rick going to do about all these unexpected visits, especially if Mallory didn't know about them?

He had to admit, though, it was a little flattering.

Lucas seemed to like him. At least, they had a shared interest in the animals. Would that continue once he learned the truth? Would he be happy to know that Rick was his biological father? Or would he be upset when he found out that Rick hadn't agreed to be a part of his early years, as Mallory had been?

Would he be angry when he found out she'd lied to him?

Mallory feared he would be, and Rick wouldn't blame him for that. What kid wouldn't? Rick had been lied to enough times in the past to distrust most of the adults in his life.

"Tell him I'll be right there," Rick said as he made a note in the file he'd been reading, then set it aside.

After getting up from his seat, he followed Kara to the empty waiting room, where Lucas was studying the tropical fish in the tank.

When the boy heard their footsteps, he turned and grinned. "Hi, Dr. Martinez. I hope you don't mind that I came by. If you would have had a bunch of people here, I would have waited and come back later."

The boy, who looked so much like Joey had when he'd looked at Rick with bright, adoring eyes, offered him a heartwarming smile.

Would his curiosity and interest in animals abate once he learned who Rick really was? Or would it escalate, causing him to stop by more often?

Was that something Mallory pondered, too?

Probably. And it no doubt concerned her.

"Does your mother know you're here?" Rick asked.

"She knows that I'm riding my bike in the neighborhood."

Something told Rick that wasn't going to be good enough. "All right, but why don't you give her a call—just to let her know exactly where you are. I don't want you to get into trouble."

Rick didn't want to be on the receiving end of her anger, either. She'd been so worried about Lucas yesterday that she'd lashed out at both of them.

"Come with me. You can use this phone to call her." Rick led the boy to Kara's desk, then watched as he dialed Mallory's number and waited until she'd answered.

"Hi, Mom. I'm at the clinic with Dr. Martinez, and he made me call so you wouldn't get mad at us."

The boy paused for a moment, listening to Mallory's response.

"Okay. I'll tell him." Lucas glanced at the waiting room. "I'm not bothering him. There isn't anyone here except for his nurse and the animals that live with him." The boy waited a beat, then nodded. "Okay."

After telling his mother that he loved her, he hung up the phone.

"So what did she say?" Rick asked.

"She said to thank you for having me call. And then she told me to make sure I'm not bothering you. Am I?"

If Rick would have had patients waiting, it might have been inconvenient. But then again, if Lucas was willing to hang out until after office hours, it wouldn't be that bad.

"When does she want you home?" Rick asked.

"Before dark. That's when we eat. And we're having tacos tonight. That's my favorite food."

Rick didn't blame him for wanting to be on time for supper—especially with tacos on the menu. He glanced at his wristwatch. That didn't give the boy much time. "Why don't we go and visit Buddy while you're here."

"That would be cool. I was also hoping we could maybe take him to visit my mom someday. Maybe, if she could see him play with me, she'd realize he isn't always naughty."

Or that he always ran amuck in the neighborhood after a rain.

"Kara," Rick said, "I need you to call a carpet cleaning company and tell them to set up an appointment to meet with Mallory Dickinson. She lives at 349 Bluebonnet Lane. Buddy tracked mud up her stairway and into one of the bedrooms the other day, and I owe her a cleaning. She told me not to worry about it, but I'm going to insist."

"Okay. My sister just had her carpets cleaned. I'll ask who she used."

Rick thanked her. "Will you also reschedule that meeting I had with Stan Jeffries at the chamber of commerce? Let him know tomorrow would work better for me."

Kara told him she'd take care of it.

"That was a super good idea, Dr. Martinez."

Rick turned to Lucas. "What was?"

"Paying to get the carpet cleaned. My mom only thinks Buddy's a bad dog because of that day he ran into the house with muddy feet. But if she can't complain about his mess anymore, then she won't be mad at him. And if we take him to visit while he's on a leash and let him play in the backyard with me, she will see that he'd make a good pet."

Lucas had a point. And while Buddy was able to jump almost any fence, maybe he'd be content to stay put as long as Lucas was around.

"Why don't we take him to see your mom today?" Rick asked.

"That would be way cool!"

Well, Rick didn't know about way cool. The whole idea could certainly backfire, but Buddy needed a home with a family. And Lucas was certainly willing to take him in. Maybe, if adopting the dog would curtail Lucas's visits to the clinic, Mallory would agree, too.

Either way, if Rick showed up with the name and telephone number of the company that would clean her carpets, as well as the dog on a leash, how could she object to a playdate with a well-behaved Buddy this evening?

And if things went the way Rick hoped they would, he might even get invited to stay for a taco dinner, which beat the canned chili he'd planned to have at home.

It sounded like a win-win to him.

What could possibly go wrong?

Mallory had no more than put a lid on the seasoned beef in the skillet when a knock sounded at the door, followed by the ring of the bell.

Lucas was due home anytime, but he would have let himself in. So she turned down the flame, then, after rinsing her hands and drying them on the dishtowel on the counter, she went to see who'd stopped by at the dinner hour.

She swung open the door, only to find Rick, Lucas and that darn dog of his standing on the stoop. To say she was surprised to see the three of them together, as if dropping in for tea, was an understatement.

"Hey, Mom," Lucas said, "Me and Dr. Martinez brought Buddy over to play in the backyard for a little while. You don't mind, do you?"

Of course she minded. The last tenants hadn't kept up the yard the way they should have, and she'd promised the landlord she'd do a much better job of it. So she'd spent the entire afternoon mowing the lawn, pulling weeds and trimming shrubs. She'd just finished an hour ago, and all she needed was for that dog to track dirt across the patio she'd just washed down.

"Dr. Martinez also brought you something," Lucas added.

Mallory glanced at Rick, and the moment she looked into those dazzling blue eyes, her heart rate spiked, just as it always used to do whenever their gazes met. And in spite of her apprehension at seeing him again—and at Buddy's visit—a smile crept across her face. "You mean the good doctor brought something besides his dog?"

Rick tossed a grin right back at her, and her heart nearly shot out of her chest.

"As a matter of fact, I did." He handed her a piece of notepaper, with Sparkle Plenty Tile and Carpet Cleaners written in a feminine script, along with the contact information. "The owner's name is Burl Kimball. That's his cell number. He's expecting your call. He'll clean your carpet whenever it's convenient, then he'll bill me for it."

When his dog had made the mess, he'd offered to pay to have the carpet cleaned, but she'd been so eager to get him out of the house as quickly as she could that she'd told him it wasn't necessary.

Later, when she'd tried to vacuum after the mud had dried, a dirty residue had remained all the way up the stairs, into the guest bedroom and down again. The stain had been an annoying reminder of Rick and his dog. She'd planned to have it professionally cleaned, but her funds were limited until she landed a job.

The fact that Rick was following through on his offer to cover the cost of the cleaning, that he was accepting responsibility for his delinquent dog and that he wanted to set things to right, touched her in an unexpected way.

"Thank you," she said. "I'll give Burl a call tomorrow."

"So is it okay?" Lucas asked her.

Mallory turned to the boy, realizing he was still waiting for her to respond to his request, which she seemed to have forgotten amidst the sparking pheromones and hormones. "Is what okay?"

"If Buddy plays with me for a while."

Did that mean Rick was going to leave and then come back for the dog? That wasn't likely, so he'd probably stick around. Which meant...

What? That she'd have to entertain him while he waited? And if that were the case, they'd be stuck in that swirl of awkward emotions that threatened to spin around them until it grew to the size of a Texas twister, threatening to destroy everything in its path.

The way she saw it, her options were limited, especially if she didn't want to come across as a cranky mom who expected a Stepford child and a perfect household.

"Okay," she told Lucas, "but don't let him get into the flowerbeds. And take him through the side gate, not through the house."

"Thanks. We'll be careful." Lucas took the leash from Rick's hand, then dashed around to the back, taking the dog, with its tail wagging, with him.

So...

Let the awkwardness begin to swirl.

Mallory tucked a strand of hair behind her ear. "I... uh, need to check something on the stove."

"Whatever it is smells good. And spicy."

"Thanks. I'm making tacos tonight." She nodded toward the doorway. "You're welcome to come in, if you'd like. Unless you'd rather go around back with Lucas."

"I think it's best if he and Buddy play by themselves."

Okay, then. So it was Texas twister time. She stepped aside, letting Rick into the house. After shutting the door, she led him into the kitchen, where the aroma of beef, tomatoes, onion and chilies filled the air.

"Can I get you something to drink?" she asked. "I have soda in the fridge. I also have a bottle of wine I can open."

"Soda sounds good to me." He took a seat on one of the barstools and watched her fix him a root beer on ice.

After handing him the glass, she checked the meat on the stove.

"Is that another one of Sue Dunlop's recipes?" he asked.

"No, this is one of my own. Or rather, it's one of my mother's. She got it from Lupe, one of our neighbors in San Salvador."

Mallory's parents had been missionaries, so she'd grown up in third world countries until she was thirteen—at least, during the school years. She spent her summer breaks in Brighton Valley with her grandparents, brushing up on her English.

"So you learned more than Spanish while living in Central America," Rick said.

"Yes, I did." She glanced over her shoulder and smiled. She and Rick used to laugh about the fact that she was more fluent in Spanish than he was, even though she wasn't Hispanic and he was—at least, on his father's side.

"Would you like to stay for dinner?" she asked.

"I don't want you to think this is going to be a regular thing—me dropping by at mealtime. It's just that Lucas showed up again at the clinic this afternoon, and after the incident yesterday, when he came home late and you were worried, I thought I'd make sure he got home safely."

She turned and leaned against the counter. Then she crossed her arms and cast him a smile. "And the visit with Buddy? Whose idea was that?"

"Lucas really likes that dog. And, for what it's worth, Buddy's gotten pretty attached to him, too."

"It's not that I don't want him to have a pet, but I was hoping to get him a rabbit or a gerbil—something small that lives in a cage."

"If you could see the two of them play together, you might change your mind."

"You have a point, but I told my landlord I'd keep up the yard work. And I'm afraid a dog like Buddy will tear things up."

Rick didn't argue, and she was glad that he hadn't. The truth was, an oversize, energetic dog wasn't a good fit for them. There was a good chance she'd be working full-time soon. And Lucas was going to start school on Monday morning. Who would be at home to take care of Buddy? The poor dog would be lonely and miserable.

"Can I do something to help?" Rick asked, gesturing toward the kitchen counter.

Since his very presence alone had elevated her heart rate and caused her body temperature to rise at least a degree, it might be a good idea to assign him a chore.

But before he arrived, Mallory had prepared small bowls with chopped lettuce, tomatoes, grated cheese, sour cream and salsa. So there wasn't much left for him to do.

Still, she had to think of something that might ease the tension—and still the attraction that sparked whenever he was around.

"You can set the table while I fry the tortillas, if you'd like." She pointed to the cupboards where she stored the plates, as well as the drawer where she kept the silverware.

Yet as he moved about the kitchen, as if cycling in and out of her life, her heart beat faster and she fought the urge to fan herself.

If he mentioned anything about her rosy cheeks, she'd blame it on the heat from the stove, although she knew better.

When Rick finished the assigned chore, he asked, "What next?"

"Why don't you call Lucas inside and have him wash up for dinner."

"All right."

When Lucas came in the house, Buddy put up a fuss.

"Why can't he come in, too?" the boy asked. "He feels bad out there all by himself."

"Not while we eat," Mallory told him.

"Please?"

It was difficult not to give in to him when he gazed at her like that—his eyes sad, hopeful, pleading. But she'd never liked the idea of having animals in the house, so she held firm.

Besides, if Lucas asked again if he could keep Buddy as a pet, she could remind him of the dog's need for constant companionship and how neither of them would be home for the bulk of the weekdays, which was validation enough.

They'd no more than sat down to eat when the howling began.

"Poor Buddy," Lucas said as he stuffed his taco with beef, cheese and lettuce. And lots of tomatoes, just as Rick had done.

So they both favored tomatoes. That was one more thing they had in common—in addition to beautiful blue eyes, dark hair and olive complexions.

After Buddy let out one rather mournful cry, Lucas leaned back in his seat and frowned. "He misses me."

"He needs to stay outside," Mallory said firmly, "especially while we eat."

"But he's crying." Lucas again sought her gaze, his eyes pleading with her to reconsider.

"Actually," Rick said, "he's just trying to get his way by whining, like some kids are prone to do. Buddy might look fully grown, but he's still a puppy and has a lot to learn."

Lucas seemed to think on that awhile, then said, "I can teach him to behave."

"I'm sure you can." Rick tossed the boy a smile. "But it won't be easy. The family that adopts Buddy will need to take him to obedience training classes."

And that was yet another reason Buddy wasn't the right pet for Lucas—or the kind of project Mallory needed to tackle right now. She was still getting used to parenting full-time, and with her grandfather's illness, as well as trying to create a home for Lucas and looking forward to the nuances of another position as a social worker at a new clinic, she didn't have time to learn the proper method of disciplining a rambunctious, overgrown puppy.

"I'm sorry," Rick said. "I guess it was a bad idea to bring him here tonight. I'll take him home."

"Please, don't go," Lucas said. "I'll get a ball and throw it outside for him to play with. Maybe that'll keep him happy until we finish eating."

At this point, Mallory was willing to try just about anything. They had to get the dog to stop whining and crying before any of her new neighbors complained about the noise. "Let's try the ball first, Rick."

Lucas pushed back from the table and left the kitchen before she could blow out a sigh. Moments later, he returned with a rubber ball.

After a little maneuvering at the back door, a couple of happy barks, a few thumps and bumps, Lucas managed to throw the rubber ball all the way to the back fence. From the sound of rubber striking wood, it must have bounced across the yard, sending the dog running.

Lucas then shut the door and returned to his seat. But there was no telling how long the peace and quiet would last.

"If you guys don't have anything to do this Saturday," Rick said, "the Lazaros are having a backyard barbecue. Marie's a great cook, so the food is always awesome—and plentiful. I'm sure there will be some kids there, so Lucas would have a chance to meet someone before he starts school on Monday."

Mallory didn't know what to do with an invitation like that. Was Rick trying to ease himself into his son's life—and thus, into hers, as well? Or was he just being neighborly?

Yet she liked the idea of Lucas getting a chance to meet other children. That's why she'd been allowing him to ride his bike in the neighborhood, hoping he'd make friends. But apparently, the people who lived on their street were mostly older couples and retirees, which was probably why Lucas kept dropping by the veterinary clinic.

"A barbecue sounds fun," Lucas said. "Can we go, Mom?"

She struggled with an answer. Something about going to a barbecue with Rick and Lucas felt a little too family-like and inappropriate for a woman who was involved with another man.

But how could she say no?

"I suppose it would be all right. That is, if Dr. Martinez doesn't think the Lazaros will mind. I'd hate to be a party-crasher."

Rick tossed her another heart-stopping grin that nearly stole her breath away—and made her wish she could reel in her acceptance of the invitation.

What had she been thinking? She was practically engaged—not that she'd actually agreed to marry Brian. But he'd let her know that he had that in mind. And she hadn't told him no.

So spending time with Rick Martinez—whether it was eating tacos or at a barbecue with his friends—was only going to mean trouble of one kind or another.

Hadn't her grandfather said as much ten years ago—that getting involved with someone she knew was wrong for her from the get-go would only lead to problems in the future?

And hadn't he proven to be right?

"Hank and Marie won't mind at all," Rick said, "but I'll give them a call."

She glanced at Lucas, whose smile had put a spark

in his eyes. "Think it would be okay if I took my Play-Station?"

"Don't bother. There's always a lot going on in the Lazaros' backyard, like flag football and games of tag. You won't miss your video games—I promise."

"Cool. Thanks for inviting us."

As much as Mallory wanted to backpedal and suddenly remember an imaginary appointment or previous engagement she'd already scheduled for that exact day and hour, she couldn't disappoint Lucas. Not when she hadn't seen him this happy since before his mother's accident.

"When you make that call," Mallory said, "please ask if there's something I can bring."

"I'm sure it won't be necessary, but I'll let you know what Marie has to say."

Before she could respond, a thump and a scratch sounded at the door.

"Uh-oh," Lucas said. "I'd better go check on Buddy."

"I'll do it." Rick pushed back from the table. "You stay here and finish your dinner."

Mallory watched as Rick went to the door to check on the rascally dog, wondering if the overgrown pup would try to crash through into the kitchen, anyway.

Sure enough, when the door opened, Buddy jumped up to greet Rick, placing his muddy front paws and dirty snout on the front of his shirt.

"Uh-oh." Rick took the dog by the collar. When he turned, allowing Mallory a full glimpse of the problem at hand, she gasped.

Buddy held the green ball in his mouth, along with a beautiful begonia bloom, roots and all.

Rick glanced over his shoulder, those blue eyes filled

with remorse. "I'm sorry, Mal. I'm sure he didn't mean to dig up your plant. He was probably just going after the ball. But it looks like I'm going to owe you some time in the flower bed."

She blew out a sigh. She knew she'd have to trust her instincts when it came to letting that pesky dog be a part of her family—or even to come for a visit.

Trouble was, her instincts told her to beware of letting Rick ease his way back into her life, too. And if she didn't do something to slow things down quickly, she was going to be in a world of trouble.

Chapter Five

On Saturday afternoon, Rick drove Mallory and Lucas into town and to the quiet neighborhood where Hank and Marie Lazaro lived.

When he'd picked them up a few minutes ago, Mallory had come to the door wearing a pretty mint-colored sundress that had set off her green eyes in such a way that another man might have forgotten the many reasons their star-crossed teenage relationship had failed in the first place and why it shouldn't be resurrected. In fact, Rick was kicking himself for even asking her and Lucas to go with him to the barbecue, especially since he'd been so determined to maintain a healthy distance from the woman who'd crushed his youthful dreams and had broken his heart.

What in the world had provoked him to do such a stupid thing?

Aw, come on. Really? You don't know?

Okay. If he really wanted to dig deep and get analytical, he had a pretty good idea why the invitation had rolled off his tongue when they'd been eating tacos at her place the other night.

He'd wanted her to know that things were different now, that he actually had friends who'd become like family to him, people who'd be more apt to grace the photos on the society pages of the local newspaper, rather than be listed in the column that announced recent criminal activity or arrests made within various areas of the county.

Hank Lazaro, a retired detective with the Wexler Police Department, probably rubbed elbows with some of her grandfather's friends, including the district attorney who'd once been Reverend Dickinson's golf buddy.

Besides that, Hank and Marie also had a home that was similar to the one in which Mallory had once lived with her grandparents—although it wasn't nearly as pristine and stuffy.

Right before that knock-down/drag-out fight that had landed Rick's uncle in jail and his aunt in the hospital, Mallory had invited Rick to have dinner with her at her grandparents' house. Rick had agreed, but he'd worried about the impression he'd make on the Reverend Dickinson and his wife. Would he know which fork to use? Would he say the right things?

At seventeen, he'd been cocky and sure of himself in almost any situation on the street. But that evening, as he'd made his way up the steps to the front door of the Dickinson house, which was located behind the Brighton Valley Community Church, he'd felt completely unbalanced and out of place.

But hell, why wouldn't he feel that way? People didn't even call it a *house.* They referred to it as the *parsonage,* which made it seem holy, a place set apart and untainted by the likes of guys like Rick.

Even though Mallory had met him at the door with a sweet kiss and an everything's-going-to-be-okay smile, that uneasy feeling hadn't gone away.

In fact, the moment he'd stepped foot inside the clean and tidy abode, he'd felt as if he'd somehow dirtied the sanctuary. He might have showered, shaved and splashed on some of the best dime-store cologne he could afford, but it hadn't seemed to matter. He'd felt as though, somehow, his clothes still carried in the stench of cheap cigarette smoke and stale booze that permeated the carpets and curtains in the apartment in which he'd lived.

And while no one had really said anything, Rick would have bet hard cash—if he'd actually had more than five bucks in his wallet—against Monopoly money that the reverend and his wife hadn't been the least bit happy when Mallory had asked to bring her "boyfriend" home for dinner, although they'd both feigned tense smiles throughout.

Rick had faked a happy face the entire time, too, but he'd been miserable.

So yeah. That's why he'd asked Mallory and Lucas to attend the barbecue at the Lazaros' today—and why he'd called Hank as soon as he'd gotten home the other night to make sure it was okay to bring two guests. And just as expected, he'd been told it was more than all right.

So here they were, nearing downtown Brighton Valley, with its quaint little shops and eateries, like Darla's Cut and Curl and Caroline's Diner.

You'd think he'd feel a sense of pride, of peace, as he neared the Lazaros' house. Instead, the silence within the confines of the truck's cab was using up all the oxygen.

But why should he let that happen? What did it matter if Mallory met—or even liked—Hank and Marie? Rick had already made his mark in the community. He was no longer the same surly teen she'd once known.

But what about Lucas?

Yeah. Maybe that's why he'd really done it. He'd wanted to introduce his son to the people who meant the most to him.

Rick stole a glance at the boy who sat between him and Mallory.

Lucas had been unusually quiet on the drive, and Rick wondered why that was. He'd been so consumed by his own thoughts that he'd neglected to think about his son.

Was Lucas worried about going to a new school on Monday and not knowing anyone? He had to be.

Rick knew exactly how that felt. He'd had to do it enough times when he'd grown up.

A wave of guilt swept over him for being so self-centered. He should have been more tuned in to what the poor kid had been feeling than in stewing about old memories that were a waste of time to even think about. But since he was about to turn right onto Cottonwood Circle, he didn't have time to deal with it now. He'd just have to make up for it later.

"I've always liked this part of town," Mallory said,

as she turned to Lucas. "I used to walk along this street on my way to school each day."

"Oh, yeah? How far did you have to go?"

"Only about five blocks."

A walk in the park. When Rick went to foster care, in order to stay at Brighton Valley High and be near Mallory, he'd had to ride a city bus from his apartment complex for almost an hour, then walk about ten blocks to the school, but he kept his mouth shut. It wasn't the time to bring up the past.

After turning onto Cottonwood Circle, he proceeded down the street to the familiar two-story redbrick house, with white trim and black shutters. He pointed to the right. "This is it, but I'm going to make a U-turn and park on the other side of the street."

"It's a beautiful home," Mallory said. "Have they lived here long?"

"About forty years. They raised their daughter, Bethany, here. She's in her third year of medical school in California."

"They must be very proud."

"She's an awesome kid—brilliant, funny and beautiful on the inside and out."

Mallory studied the house again. "With it just being the two of them at home now, are they thinking about downsizing?"

"No, they're pretty social. They're always hosting get-togethers of one kind or another. I don't think they'll ever sell this place."

"Well, if they ever put it on the market," Mallory said, "I'll bet it wouldn't last very long."

"I'm sure you're right."

The house had what Realtors would call "curb appeal," a well-tended yard and lawn, along with colorful flowerbeds and a winding sidewalk bordered with marigolds that led to the front porch. But the most appealing thing of all, at least as far as Rick was concerned, was to be found inside the house. And that's what drew him back time and again.

After pulling his truck behind a white SUV, Rick shut off the ignition. "Here we are."

Mallory scanned the other vehicles parked along both sides of the curb. "I guess we're not the first to arrive. How many people are they expecting?"

"It's hard to say. I recognize a couple of cars, but I'm not sure if you'd know them. Tom Randall is here. And I think that white SUV belongs to Brad Welling."

"Do they have kids?" Lucas asked from the backseat.

"No, but when I called, I asked Hank if there would be children here, and he said there would be."

They climbed from the truck. Mallory carried the plate of brownies she'd brought.

"Are you nervous about meeting kids you don't know?" Rick asked Lucas.

"A little. But I'm more nervous about going to a new school on Monday and not knowing anyone. So it would be better to meet someone here first."

"I agree," Rick said.

They headed up the walk to the front door, where a woven, heart-shaped mat and matching pots of red geraniums welcomed them and gave visitors a sense of coming home. At least, that's the feeling Rick always got whenever he approached the house, crossed the threshold and caught a whiff of whatever Marie was baking or cooking.

He'd never experienced the like at any of the other

places he'd ever lived, including the apartment behind the clinic where he now hung his hat.

"Can I ring the doorbell?" Lucas asked.

"Sure," Rick said. "Go ahead."

Moments later, the door swung open, and they were met by Hank, who greeted Rick with a firm handshake, followed by a manly hug. "It's good to see you, and to welcome your friends."

"This is Mallory Dickinson and…" Rick looked at the boy, wanting more than anything to acknowledge their actual relationship in front of the man he admired and respected most in the world. But he and Mallory had an agreement he intended to keep. "And this is her son, Lucas."

Mallory shuffled the plate of brownies into the crook of her left arm so she could shake hands with her host.

"It's nice to meet you," Hank said as he greeted her with a warm and firm grip. "Marie and I are so happy you came."

"Thanks for allowing us to tag along."

"It's our pleasure. We love having company. Our rule of thumb has always been the more the merrier, especially for barbecues."

The retired detective, who appeared to be in his mid- to late sixties, wasn't a big man—just five-eight or nine—yet he seemed to be large in every other sense of the word—a deep commanding voice, broad shoulders and a stocky stance.

"Rick said that it wasn't necessary to bring anything," Mallory said, glancing down at the plastic-wrapped plate of goodies in her arms. "But I was making a batch of brownies to thank my neighbor for watching Lucas for me and doubled the recipe. I didn't want to come empty-handed."

"They look delicious." Hank splayed his hand over his rounded belly. "And while I'm sure we'll have plenty to eat today, I love chocolate, so I can guarantee they won't last long."

As Hank stepped aside, they entered the house, and Rick closed the door behind them.

"Come with me," Hank said, as he led them through a cozy living room with dark, distressed wood floors, leather furniture and a large LCD television mounted to the wall.

They moved through so quickly that Mallory didn't have a chance to check out the decor, the artwork on the walls or the photographs on the fireplace mantel, but she did notice a warm, homey vibe.

On the other hand, they stopped in the kitchen, which was spacious and functional, with red walls, gray granite countertops and stainless-steel appliances. Splashes of yellow and green in the artwork, which was a chicken and barnyard decor, made the room bright and cheery.

A petite older woman was slicing tomatoes and preparing burger fixings at an island in the center of the room. She glanced up and smiled as they joined her.

"Honey," Hank said. "Rick and Mallory are here."

Marie Lazaro, an attractive woman, with plump rosy cheeks and her salt-and-pepper-colored hair pulled into a topknot, brightened and set the knife on the counter. After wiping her hands on a red-and-white-checkered dishtowel, she greeted Rick with a hug.

Then she turned to Mallory and Lucas, her brown eyes welcoming and expressive, her smile warm. "I'm so glad you came."

"Thanks so much for including us," Mallory said.

"You really didn't need to bring anything, but it was nice that you did. Don't those brownies look yummy." Marie reached for the platter. "Let's set them over here."

"Is there anything I can do to help?" Mallory asked.

"Well…" Marie glanced at the counter, where she had a head of iceberg lettuce, a red onion and a package of American cheese slices. "If you don't mind, I could actually use a little help. I'd meant to prepare this stuff earlier, but I received a call from a troubled friend who needed an ear. And it set me back a bit this morning."

"Why don't I take Lucas out in the backyard with me," Hank said. "I'll introduce him to Jason and Ryan, the kids who've been staying with Tom. I'll bet he'd like to play catch with them, too."

"Good idea," Marie said.

Tom Randall was another one of Hank's success stories. Once a teenager prone to trouble, much like Rick, Tom was now a local cattle rancher who also bred cutting horses.

As Hank led Lucas out the sliding door and into the backyard, Rick asked Marie, "Who are Tom's houseguests?"

"Actually, I think it might be more permanent than that. Did I tell you that Tom has been involved in my church outreach program?"

Rick nodded.

"Well, a few months ago, he met the boys while we were volunteering our time in a poor area of Potter's Junction, a small town about fifty miles from here." Marie scanned the windows and doorways. It appeared to be clear, but she lowered her voice anyway. "They're good kids who'd been living with various family members and moving from home to home. They never knew whose sofa they'd be sleeping on next. And as a result, they were struggling in school. It was a pretty sad situation."

Unable to help herself, Mallory glanced at Rick, saw the furrow in his brow, the tightening of his lips.

"We were going to report them to protective services, but Tom asked us to hold off. The kids weren't in imminent danger. They just weren't being loved and cared for properly."

"Why did he want you to wait?" Rick asked.

"He invited them out to his house for the weekend, and the kids had a great time. So he did it again the following week, only that time he picked them up on Friday after school and returned them to school on Monday morning. Then he asked how they'd like to move in with him. The kids were thrilled, and since none of those families really wanted to take them in—or even had a legal claim to them, anyway—Tom went to social services and became their foster parent. He's only had them a couple of weeks, but they seem to be doing well."

"I haven't seen Tom in a while," Rick said. "I think I'll head outside and talk to him."

Mallory wondered if he was more curious about the boys, whose lives might have been worse than his own. Or maybe he wanted to see how Lucas was relating to them. She had to admit, she was curious, too.

After Rick left the kitchen, she thanked Marie again for allowing her and Lucas to come. "It's especially nice because we're new to the neighborhood, and my son will be starting school on Monday. I'd hoped he'd meet some other children while we were here."

"I can't remember their exact ages, but I think one

of Tom's boys is in second grade, and the other is in third or fourth."

"That's perfect."

"Can I get you something to drink?" Marie asked. "Water, iced tea, fruit punch? Maybe a glass of sangria? It's Hank's special recipe."

Mallory smiled. "I'll start with the iced tea and try the sangria later."

Marie smiled, then reached into the cupboard for a glass. "Rick tells us that you're Reverend Dickinson's granddaughter."

Rick had told her that he and the Lazaros were close. What else had he told Hank and Marie about her—and Lucas?

Rather than make any assumptions—or offer up any detailed information about the past, she asked a question of her own. "Yes, I am. How do you know my grandfather?"

"I have a couple of friends who go to Brighton Valley Community Church, and they've always spoken very highly of him. He's very well respected in town. I heard that he's been ill and had to retire. I hope he's doing better."

"He had bypass surgery a few weeks ago, but his diabetes and other health issues complicated his recovery for a while, which is why I decided to move back. Fortunately, he's finally on the mend. He's still at the Brighton Valley Medical Center now, but they're talking about discharging him. He'll need nursing assistance, but they have that available in the senior complex where he lives."

"It's nice that he has you here to help coordinate things for him," Marie said.

"I just wish I would have moved home sooner. After Gram died, I suggested doing so, but he said it wasn't necessary. The board of elders had just hired a new pastor, and he planned to cut back on his responsibilities. He also moved out of the parsonage at that time and into a small apartment. He insisted that he was happy and that his friends from church kept him busy. I believed him, but..."

"I'm sure that was true," Marie said. "You had a life in Boston. You couldn't very well move back to Brighton Valley just because your grandmother died."

"No, but..."

There was so much Marie didn't know, so much Mallory wouldn't share. Yet Marie was sure to learn all about it soon—once Rick was free to tell the world that Lucas was actually his son. And once the entire town knew the real reason Mallory had moved to Boston.

"It's all very complicated," Mallory said. "My parents were missionaries and died in an accident in San Salvador when I was thirteen. So I spent my teenage years with my grandparents, and we were very close. So I feel badly about being away from Grandpa for so long. But I'm back now, hoping to make up for being away."

Marie reached over and placed her hand on Mallory's arm. "When we open our hearts to love and forgiveness, things have a way of working out just the way they're supposed to—and in the proper time."

Even when we mess up? Mallory wanted to ask the woman. But a question like that was far too heavy to discuss with a woman she'd only met minutes ago. In fact, she'd rather avoid the entire topic altogether, no matter how easy Marie Lazaro was to talk to.

Several minutes later, after preparing and refrigerating a platter of lettuce leaves and slices of tomatoes, onions, pickles and cheese, Marie helped Mallory tidy up the countertops, then the women went outside.

Carrying her glass of iced tea, Mallory made her way across the patio to the shade of a tree, where Lucas sat with the other boys, sipping on colas, a baseball and two mitts resting beside them. Jason and Ryan, who resembled each other, with wheat-colored hair, green eyes and freckled noses, were close enough in age that they could have passed for twins.

It pleased her to see Lucas making friends, especially with kids who went to the same school he'd be attending, even if they might not be in the same class.

"I hope you don't have Mrs. Carson," the smaller boy was saying. "She's mean. And no one likes her."

"Yeah," the bigger boy added. "It's too bad Dylan Jessup isn't in her class. He's always picking on everyone, and he deserves a teacher like her. Instead, he got Miss Ryan, and she's super nice."

Mallory wished the kids would sing the praises of Brighton Valley Elementary, rather than tell Lucas all the things they didn't like about it.

"Hi," she said, as she approached.

"Hey, Mom." Lucas pointed to the boy at his right. "This is Jason. And the other guy is his brother, Ryan."

"It's nice to meet you." Mallory took a sip of her tea, then offered them a friendly smile. "So tell me. What's your favorite thing to do at school?"

"I like recess," the smaller boy—Ryan—said. "We play soccer and stuff like that."

"Art is fun, too," Jason said. "And we get to go to the library and eat ice cream on Fridays."

"That sounds pretty cool to me," Mallory said,

watching Lucas, hoping he agreed. His first day of school would be here before they knew it, and she didn't want him to experience any Monday-morning jitters. "What do you play at recess?"

The boys answered, and as Lucas chimed in, she decided the kids' conversation was back on a more positive track. So she excused herself and headed toward a couple of empty patio chairs that rested near an elm tree.

Moments later, Marie approached carrying a glass of iced tea. "Mind if I join you?"

"Not at all. Please do."

Marie settled into the chair beside Mallory. "It looks as though the kids have hit it off."

"Yes, they have."

They watched the boys for a moment, saw them chuckle about something Lucas had said. Mallory was glad to know he had a sense of humor. It would come in handy when it came time to make new friends on Monday.

"Lucas is a beautiful child."

"Thank you."

"He must keep you busy."

"He does, especially now that we're trying to settle into a new house. I'm also looking for work, so I've had to shuffle him to the sitter a lot, but he's a good sport about it."

"What kind of job are you looking for?"

"Something in social services. I have a degree in social work. I've applied at several places, mostly in Wexler, but I'm hopeful I'll land a position at the Brighton Valley Medical Center. I'm hoping they call me back for a second interview."

"That sounds promising."

"I think so, too. Working there would be my first choice, so we'll see what happens. I hope to hear something this week."

"I'll say a prayer for you—and think positive thoughts."

"I'd appreciate that. Thank you."

A man whistled, and Mallory glanced across the lawn, realizing that the men had gathered there and were calling the boys to join them in a game of flag football. Lucas, Ryan and Jason quickly jumped up, clearly delighted to be included.

"How did you and Rick meet?" Marie asked.

So Rick hadn't told her? Or did she already have Rick's story and was trying to get Mallory's side of it?

Had she noted that Lucas didn't resemble Mallory at all? And that he looked a lot like Rick?

"We went to high school together," Mallory said. "And when I moved back to town, I learned that his veterinary clinic was just down the street. We've sort of…reconnected."

"That's nice."

Was it? Mallory wasn't so sure about that. Her feelings kept vacillating between nice and terribly inconvenient.

Had Marie noticed that she kept scanning the yard, looking for Rick? And that she'd often find him gazing at her?

Was Marie curious about why Rick had asked Mallory and Lucas to join him? Was she full of questions? Was she suspicious?

Still, Mallory liked Marie. And the woman didn't seem gossipy—just genuinely concerned and caring.

"It's refreshing to see men interacting with kids like that," Mallory said.

"Hank and I wouldn't have it any other way."

"You must love children."

"We do. When we got married, we wanted to have a house full of them. But we weren't able to have any of our own. So we found ways to create a family."

"Your daughter Bethany is adopted?"

Marie nodded. "She was nearly two when we brought her home from China. But we also consider every one of these young men one of our kids, too. And, at least for today, you and Lucas are part of our brood."

"Thank-you. I appreciate that." And as she watched her son run out for a pass, a big old smile pasted on his face, she truly did. It was the happiest she'd seen him in a long time—at least, since Sue had died.

And interestingly enough, for the next couple of hours, Mallory felt like a part of the Lazaro family, too.

While seated on lawn chairs in the shade of an elm that grew in the Lazaros' backyard, Rick, Mallory and Lucas ate together. But as soon as Lucas had finished two hot dogs and chugged down most of his punch, he ditched the adults to play with his newfound friends.

"It's nice to see him having fun with the other boys," Mallory said. "I haven't heard him laugh like that in a long time."

"I figured he'd have a good time," Rick said.

"You know, I felt a little uneasy about coming today, but you were right. Hank and Marie are really nice. And it's been so good for Lucas. I'm glad we came."

Rick knew what she meant. He'd had second thoughts after inviting her and Lucas to join him, too, although he wouldn't admit it.

It wasn't as though he'd dreaded being around his old

high school flame. On the contrary, he found himself drawn to her. And that was the problem.

They'd made some bad decisions in the past—at least, *he* had. And now, ten years later, the choices he'd made as a teenager were staring him down—as if there were something he should or could do to make it all right.

He could do something about Lucas, of course, even if he wasn't quite sure where or how to begin. But there wasn't much he could do about Mallory—or the dreams he'd once had of creating a life together with her.

As he focused his attention on their son, the oldest of Tom Randall's boys threw a pass, and Lucas ran to catch it, snagging it before it landed in Marie's rose garden.

After a few hoots and cheers, the kids came together in a huddle. Then they trotted over to where Tom was talking to Hank.

"Lucas is going to be a good athlete," Rick said. "He's quick on his feet and has good hands."

"He's bright, too," Mallory added. "He was in the gifted class in Boston."

A surge of pride darn near lifted Rick off his seat, even though his only paternal contribution to his point had been a matter of genetics.

Still, when Lucas jogged over to him and Mallory, his blue eyes bright, a smile plastered on his face, Rick couldn't help feeling almost like a real parent—and the dad in a family of three.

"That was a good catch," Mallory said.

Lucas brightened even more. "You saw it?"

Before either parent could respond, Tom's oldest boy ran up and asked, "Hey, Lucas, do you wanna come to the ranch and ride horses with us?"

The younger boy, who'd been on his heels, chimed in. "Yeah! Ask your mom and dad if it's okay."

Lucas looked at Rick, then at the other boys and chuckled. "This isn't my dad. This is Dr. Martinez. He's just our neighbor and our friend."

Just? Rick wasn't sure what he'd expected. But he suddenly felt as inconsequential as a leaky balloon three days after a birthday party.

Still, Jason and Ryan merely took one last gander at Rick, then shook off the confusion with a shrug and accepted the explanation as fact.

"Then is it okay with your mom?" the younger boy asked.

Lucas turned to Mallory, his eyes pleading with her to say yes.

"We'll see," she said. "I'll have to talk to Tom."

"Cool." Lucas turned to his new friends. "Come on. Let's go."

The boys had no more than run off when Tom Randall sauntered up to Rick and Mallory and issued the invitation himself.

"Jason and Ryan would like Lucas to come to the ranch," Tom said. "It would be nice if you two brought him out for the day. We could have a picnic by the lake. It's probably too cold for the kids to swim, but they could fish. Or they could just run around and play."

Mallory, her cheeks flushed, didn't answer right away.

Rick figured it was because the invitation had gone out to them as a family unit.

Was she that uneasy being paired up as a couple with him?

"Lucas and I are going to be pretty busy for a while

with school and my job interviews," she finally said. "So I can't commit to anything now. But it certainly sounds like fun. We'll have to do that someday."

Someday.

It was one of those noncommittal words a polite person offered when they didn't want to commit to anything. But Rick was okay with that. He knew where he stood with her—where he'd always stood.

"All right, then." Tom offered Mallory a smile, but he took a step back, as if taking the hint that she wasn't going to get locked into a visit. He nodded toward the kids. "We can talk more about it later. I've got to get back to the ranch, so I need to tell the boys it's time to go."

Talk about awkward moments.

But if Mallory thought she could keep their relationship a secret, she was wrong.

Fortunately, if anyone here today had guessed that Lucas was actually Rick's son, they'd had the good sense and decency to keep that thought to themselves.

While Tom walked away, Rick said, "We'd better take off, too. I have to feed the animals."

"Good idea. There are a few things I need to do, too." Mallory got to her feet. Then she picked up the empty paper plates and used plasticware and headed toward the house.

As she walked away, Rick scanned the yard, looking for any trash the kids might have left behind.

Attending the barbecue at the Lazaros' house might have been good for Lucas, but as far as Rick was concerned, it had been a one-shot deal. He wasn't going to include Lucas and Mallory in any more family-style events.

He was even more convinced that his decision had been the right one when Marie took him aside and made the comment that he knew she'd been dying to say ever since she first laid eyes on Lucas.

"It's amazing how much Mallory's son resembles you," she said.

"Yeah, isn't it?"

"Mallory said you met at Brighton Valley High."

Rick didn't respond. Instead, he picked up two plastic cups nearly full of punch the kids hadn't finished.

"I saw the way you kept stealing glances at her," Marie added. "And she kept looking at you, too. It's obvious that whatever you felt for each other is still burning bright."

Rick forced a smile and chuckle. "You're imagining things. We're just friends."

In fact, it could even be argued that they no longer had any kind of relationship at all.

Marie placed a gentle hand on Rick's back. "It's not easy to get over your first love."

At that, he actually laughed, although he thought it might have come out a little hollow. "I'm afraid you've been watching too much of the Hallmark Channel. Besides, Mallory has a boyfriend."

Then he headed for the house before she could share any more of her observations with him. Because no matter what she sensed, what she thought she saw, he'd never stood a chance with Mallory.

Her grandfather was a retired minister, for goodness' sake. And Rick had always suspected that the old man thought even the high school valedictorian, who'd gone to Harvard, wouldn't have been good enough for her.

So Rick was back to plan A, which was to distance

himself from Mallory for a while. He'd take her and Lucas home, then pour himself into his work.

Maybe next weekend, they could tell Lucas together that Rick was his father. Then Rick could begin to build some kind of relationship with his son—minus Mallory, of course.

It was a good plan. And one that he vowed to stick to.

That is, until he strode through the sliding door and into the Lazaros' kitchen, just as Mallory was walking out.

And *bam!*

They ran smack dab into each other with a thump, throwing her completely off balance and splattering red punch all over.

She probably ought to thank her lucky stars—or maybe he ought to thank his—that he grabbed her, because she might have fallen to the ground if he hadn't.

And for a moment, as he held her in his arms, as he inhaled her soft, floral scent, as their gazes locked, the years rolled away and they were kids again—hearts racing, hormones pumping—and with eyes only for each other.

Chapter Six

Mallory's pulse raced dangerously out of control, and not only because of her collision with Rick and her near fall to the floor. It was because she'd found herself wrapped in his embrace, his forearm tucked under her breast, his breath warm against her ear, his musky scent filling her lungs, squeezing the heart right out of her.

"I'm sorry," he said.

About what? Saving her from a fall? Or running into her and nearly causing her to fall in the first place?

She blinked, regaining her thoughts and her senses, then straightened.

"Don't slip," he said, as he slowly released her and helped her stand upright. "There's punch all over the floor."

She glanced down at the two empty plastic cups, as well as the red liquid pooled on the ceramic tile. Then, as her gaze lifted, she noticed the bright red splatter that ran the length of Rick's white button-down shirt, which had looked sharp and been crisply pressed when he'd picked her and Lucas up earlier today.

"Oh, no," she said. "That stain is going to set if you don't treat it right away."

"I'll soak it when I get home. At least we managed to keep it off your dress."

He said it as if he'd gone to great measures to take the spill on her behalf, although she doubted that was the case.

Or had he? He'd certainly kept her from falling.

She took another look at his shirt. Cold water alone wasn't going to do it. She wondered what kind of stain remover he had, although she supposed that was the least of her problems.

Truly, all she really wanted to do was to go home, as they'd been planning to do when this unfortunate collision had occurred, and forget the way her body still reacted to Rick's touch.

When Marie came along with a roll of paper towels, as well as a wet rag, Mallory stepped out of the way. The older woman quickly cleaned up the spill, all the while making light of the incident and the resulting mess.

And in the scheme of things, it wasn't that big of a deal. *Really.*

Yet Mallory's heart continued to tumble in her chest as if it was trying to make sense of it all, the arousing zing of Rick's touch, the blood-stirring allure of his scent....

She really needed to shake it off.

"Is there something I can do to help?" Mallory asked, thinking that her pulse rate would go back to normal if she had a job to do, one that removed her from Rick's immediate proximity.

"No, not a thing," Marie said. "Hank and I have our party cleanup down to a science."

So, after saying a second goodbye, Rick and Mallory gathered up Lucas, who'd made plans to meet Jason and Ryan near the handball court before the first bell rang on Monday morning, then they headed for Rick's truck and started the short trip home.

The drive back to her house was quiet and solemn. She had no idea what was on Rick's mind, but she couldn't help wondering if they were pondering the same things—the family time they'd spent while eating, the intimacy of the collision in the kitchen.

What was going on?

When we open our hearts to love and forgiveness, things have a way of working out just the way they're supposed to.

Was there something to what Marie had said? Did beauty actually come from ashes?

When they arrived at Mallory's house, they got out of the truck, and Rick walked them to the front door— just as though they'd been on a date.

No, *not* like a date. They'd had Lucas with them. They'd taken him to meet some new friends so his first day of school would go easier. It had all been very innocent and platonic.

"Thanks for taking us to the barbecue," Lucas said. "I really liked your friends, Dr. Martinez."

"You're welcome. I'm glad you went with me and that you enjoyed the kids and people you met."

They paused on the stoop, and as Mallory looked at Rick, she couldn't help but notice the bright red splat-

ter of punch that marred his shirt and felt a bit responsible for it being there.

She unlocked the front door. "Lucas, why don't you
go inside and take a shower."

"Why?" he asked.

"Because it's time for you to clean up and to wind
down for the day. If you do it now, we can make some
popcorn and watch a movie together this evening."

He seemed to think about that for a moment, then
relented. "Okay."

After saying goodbye to Rick, Lucas went in the
house.

"Thanks again for inviting us today. You were right
about the Lazaros. I'm glad I had a chance to meet
them."

Rick tossed her a boyish grin. "Yeah, well, I thought
that if you knew I had better friends these days it might
make you feel better about letting Lucas spend time
with me."

She returned his smile. "I'd already made that assumption."

There it went again, that annoying awkwardness
that settled over them whenever they were alone. Well,
Mallory would just have to chase it off by ending their
day. But as her gaze drifted down to the red punch drying into the white fabric of his shirt, she had second
thoughts about an immediate escape.

"You know," she said, "I have an awesome laundry
product that works on all kinds of stains. Why don't
you let me wash that shirt for you?"

"You don't have to do that."

No, she didn't. But it seemed like the right thing to
offer, the natural thing to suggest.

"You paid for the mess your dog made on my carpet," she explained. "And I have to admit, I should have noticed you coming through that doorway with those plastic cups in your hand."

"Are you sure?" he asked. "You don't mind?"

What would a simple act of neighborly kindness hurt?

"No, I don't mind at all."

"Okay." He began to pull the shirttails out of the waistband of his pants. "I can come by for it tomorrow—or whenever it's convenient."

Washing his shirt was one thing, but having Rick stop by on Sunday was another. Knowing Lucas, he'd invite the good animal doctor to stay for dinner, and she couldn't allow things to get any cozier between the three of them than they already had.

"Tomorrow won't work," she said. "I'm going to visit my grandfather. They're talking about discharging him, so I'm going to spend the afternoon making sure his apartment is ready and that he has the nursing assistance he's going to need. Why don't I drop off the shirt on Monday morning, after I take Lucas to school?"

"All right. But I feel a little weird undressing out here."

She didn't blame him for that. "Come on inside. You can use the downstairs bathroom."

Once he'd entered the living room, she pointed out the door he should use. Rick began to unbutton his shirt, starting at the top and going down until it opened all the way. She watched, almost mesmerized, until he disappeared into the bathroom.

Moments later, he stepped out, tall, lean and barechested. Rick Martinez had definitely grown up and filled out in the nicest way. And as he handed her the stained shirt, her tummy clenched and an ache settled deep in her core.

A familiar ache.

An unwelcome ache.

Why hadn't she volunteered to pick up his shirt on Monday? Allowing him to leave it here tonight and letting him go home half-dressed had been a bad idea. A very bad idea.

She took the shirt from him, then nodded toward the door. "I'd better check on Lucas. And I'll drop the shirt off at your office when it's clean."

"All right. I'll see you Monday."

She told him goodbye, and as soon as he stepped outside, she shut the door before she did something crazy like ask him if he wanted a cup of coffee or a glass of wine.

What good could possibly come from that?

She paused in the center of the living room, the memories of today blurring with those of a lifetime.

For some reason, Marie's words again came to mind. *When we open our hearts to love and forgiveness, things have a way of working out just the way they're supposed to.*

As nice as that had sounded, and as much as Mallory might wish that it could be true, things didn't always work out the way they were supposed to.

When Mallory had lived with her missionary parents in San Salvador, she'd spent each summer with her grandparents in Brighton Valley. But one July day, that vacation became permanent when they received word that her parents had died in a flash flood that had swept their car into a raging river.

Mallory had been heartbroken, and while love and faith had seen her through, it was impossible to believe that her parents were supposed to die. That she was supposed to be orphaned and live in Brighton Valley.

That she was meant to meet Rick, to conceive Lucas...

And what about the Dunlops? Had she been meant to give her baby up to them?

And what about their deaths?

No, all those losses were too hurtful and too complicated to consider.

Sometimes bad things happened to good people.

And sometimes good people made bad mistakes—and then they were forced to live with the consequences.

Marie Lazaro had been wrong. Mallory and Rick weren't destined to be together. Too much had happened in the past ten years to roll back the clock and start over.

Mallory had no idea how long she'd stood in the center of living room, pondering things best left in the past. Long enough that she ought to check on Lucas.

She'd no more than started up the stairs when her cell phone rang. She retrieved it from her purse, then checked the display.

It was Brian. She hadn't talked to him since yesterday morning, when he'd left for a weeklong fishing trip in the mountains with his brother, so she really ought to be happy to hear from him. Yet instead of the warm, comfy feeling she usually got whenever he called, an uneasy, guilt-laden shiver tore through her.

She did her best to shrug it off, though. After all, she hadn't done anything wrong. So she greeted him, then asked about his trip.

"It's been awesome so far," he said. "I just came

into town to pick up some stuff and to check email at a coffee shop with Wi-Fi, since the cabin is so remote. How are you?"

"We're doing well. Lucas and I went to a barbecue this afternoon, and he met two boys who attend his new school. So that should make his adjustment much easier."

"That's good. I'm glad you're getting out and meeting people."

Another wave of guilt swept over her, probably because of who she'd been with, as well as the fact that she'd never gotten around to telling Brian about Rick— or correcting his belief that the man was dead.

But she certainly couldn't put that off any longer. Not when he'd been so good to her, so supportive, so understanding and patient.

"Listen, Brian. I need to tell you something." Mallory walked into the kitchen in an attempt to find some privacy. Even after shutting the door, she lowered her voice. "Lucas has been under the impression that his biological father died."

"And he didn't?"

"No. A couple of years ago, soon after Gary passed away, Lucas asked me about his 'other dad' and wanted to know how we could find him. I think he wanted to fill the hole Gary's death left in his heart. And he thought he could have a relationship with Rick, much like the one he had with me. But Rick hadn't wanted any part of an open adoption. In fact, he'd been adamantly opposed to it. I'd also been unsure of the kind of person Rick had become, so I decided to protect Lucas from the truth."

"So you *lied* to him?"

She winced at the reality. A part of her wanted to explain, but she doubted there was any use in trying to defend herself.

Would it matter that everything else she'd told the grieving little boy had been true? That she and her grandparents had thought that she'd been too young to raise a baby on her own?

When talking to Lucas that day, she'd told him how she'd asked God to help her find the perfect parents for him. And that He'd led her to the Dunlops, who'd been praying for a little boy just like him.

Then, after nearly twenty hours of labor, Mallory had given birth to a beautiful six pound, three ounce baby boy who would be known as Lucas Scott Dunlop. She'd held her son all too briefly, then, with a heavy heart and tears in her eyes, she handed the precious bundle to Sue Dunlop.

No, she doubted that any of that would matter to anyone—her grandfather, Rick or even to Brian.

"Bottom line?" she said, tears welling in her eyes again. "Yes, I lied to Lucas. I thought sparing him from the truth was the best thing to do at the time, but now I realize I was wrong."

"What about me?" Brian asked. "Why'd you let me believe that the guy was dead? You could have told me sooner."

Yes, she could have. And she didn't blame Brian for being annoyed, especially when he'd been more than patient with her for the past six months.

He'd asked her to marry him just weeks before Sue's death, and she'd told him she'd think about it. But after the accident, she and Lucas had both been devastated. Brian had tried to console her and had wanted to help, but Mallory had told him that Lucas needed her undivided attention for the time being, and that while he was grieving, he had to come first.

Brian had said that he understood, and he'd given her the space she'd needed, which meant they'd pretty much put their relationship on hold.

They'd just started to see each other again, although Lucas didn't seem to be too happy about having to share Mallory. And then Grandpa had suffered the heart attack, and she'd decided to move to Brighton Valley.

Poor Brian hadn't signed on for any of this. And she felt to blame, even though she hadn't signed on for it, either.

"I'm sorry," she said. "I never meant to deceive you. I'd planned to tell you what I'd told Lucas and why, but I never got around to it because I got so caught up with the move. And since I hadn't heard from Rick in more than nine years, I assumed he'd probably left town, like his brother had. Or that he was in jail or worse. And talking about him just didn't seem to be a priority since I didn't think there was any chance we'd ever run into him." She paused for a moment, and when Brian didn't say anything, she added, "The good news is, at least as far as Lucas is concerned, Rick has turned his life around and is respected in the community."

"Bully for him."

Brian was angry. Or maybe he was jealous. He might even be both.

After a beat, Brian asked, "So what does he do for a living?"

"He's a veterinarian."

Silence crept over the line again, and while she was

tempted to say something, she didn't know what more to add.

"Has Lucas met him yet?"

"Yes, but he doesn't know who he really is. I'll have to tell him, of course. But I haven't done that yet."

More of the dreaded silence. Then Brian asked, "How did you run into him?"

"His clinic is just down the street from the house I rented. And I met him when he was out walking his dog."

"Are you okay with that?"

"What do you mean?"

"Having your old lover so close."

He seemed to be probing and prying for more information than she was telling him. But there wasn't much more to say.

Or was there?

She cleared her throat. "We've talked some. And things are cordial. It's fine."

"Good." Again he paused. Then, as if he didn't want to talk about Rick any more than she did, he switched topics. "Any news on the job hunt?"

"I'm hoping to hear something from the Brighton Valley Medical Center soon. They might want a second interview, although the first one went so well, that it's possible one was enough. But even if they tell me that they've decided to hire someone else, I haven't stopped filling out applications or sending out my resume."

"I'm sure you'll get that position. The HR department at the medical center would be crazy not to hire you with your qualifications—and your personality."

"Thanks." She appreciated having someone in her corner, someone who believed in her. When she'd lived in Boston, when she'd been afraid to share news of her achievements and promotions with her grandfather because it would only remind him of how far away she'd moved, Brian's praise and support had become especially valuable.

"I have some good news, too, honey. It looks like my transfer to the Wexler office is going to go through. If things work out the way I think they will, I'll be moving to Brighton Valley within the next two months."

Her heart thumped.

"Aren't you going to say anything?" he asked.

"I'm…stunned."

"I told you it would go through without a hitch. Didn't you believe me?"

"Yes, of course. It's just so…soon."

"*Soon*? It seems like we've been apart for ages," he said.

Did it? She'd been so busy with the move, with the job hunt, with her grandfather and with Lucas, that she'd…well, that she'd put their relationship on the back burner—again.

"I mean, it's so much sooner than I'd expected." She glanced at the stained shirt in her hand. "I had no idea that things would come together so quickly."

"There's still a lot to do. I have things I want to pack and put into storage. I also took some extra vacation time so that I could fly out to Texas a week from Monday. I'm going to need to find a place to live. I can get a hotel, although I'd like to stay with you while I'm in town—if that's okay."

Stay with her? No, that wasn't going to work. She knew that it might be a logical assumption for him to make. But life in a small town was different from what it was like in the city. At least, it was for her.

"I'm afraid that's not all right, Brian. I told you about my grandfather—about how conservative he is. He'd be upset if I were to let you move in with me."

More than that, there was also Lucas to consider. What kind of example would that set for him? She didn't want him to think she didn't value marriage, especially since she hadn't married his father.

Then, to top it all off, Lucas still didn't know that Rick was his biological father, which was one more hurdle they'd have to get over. And with Rick now in the picture—

"Mom!" Lucas called from upstairs. "I have a problem!" His voice grew louder as he approached the kitchen. "I forgot and left the water on again. And now it's all over the bathroom floor."

Oh, for Pete's sake. Mallory blew out a sigh, then hurried out the door to meet Lucas, the shirt still in one hand, the cell phone pressed to her ear with the other.

"Listen Brian, I need to hang up. I'll talk to you later this evening."

"I'm heading back to the cabin shortly, and there isn't any reception there. I'll have to talk to you next time I'm in town—maybe Monday or Tuesday. I'll double-check my itinerary and let you know what time my flight arrives in Houston and when you can expect me in Brighton Valley."

After ending the call, she stuffed the cell phone in her pocket, then hurried up the stairs, the crumpled shirt still in her hand.

She'd told Rick she'd get the stain out for him—and she would. But what about the other mess, the one she'd found herself in when Rick Martinez had walked back into her life?

Too bad they didn't make a handy-dandy stain remover for messes like that.

On Monday morning, after kissing Lucas goodbye and wishing him the best day ever, Mallory dropped him off at his new school, then drove to the veterinary clinic. It had taken a little more effort than she'd thought, but she'd managed to get the stain out of Rick's shirt, which was now neatly pressed and hanging up in the back of her car.

She'd no more than parked and shut off the ignition when her cell phone rang. She didn't recognize the number, but it was local.

"Mallory Dickinson?" an unfamiliar female voice asked.

"Yes."

"This is Valerie Evans, the HR director at Brighton Valley Medical Center. I'm calling to offer you the social worker position."

Her heart soared at the news. "I'm glad to hear that, Valerie. I accept."

"Good. Can you come into my office this afternoon and complete some paperwork? I'd like to talk more to you about the start date and other details."

"Yes, I can do that." She'd have to find someone to pick up Lucas from school. Hopefully, Alice was available. "What time should I come in?"

"How about two-thirty?"

"That's fine. I'll see you then."

After ending the call, Mallory sat in the car for a moment, basking in the good news. Sweet! She'd landed the job.

From what she'd gathered during the interview, the start date could be as soon as a week from today. And since she wanted to make sure her grandfather was settled in his apartment before her time was taken up with the job, she had a lot to do—and not much time to do it. So she'd better get busy.

She checked her hair and lipstick in the rearview mirror, then scolded herself. She'd just left the house fifteen minutes ago. It's not as if she'd been caught in a windstorm.

Besides, what did it matter how she looked? No way was she going to start primping for Rick Martinez.

She reached for her purse, then paused to scan the empty parking lot. Maybe the clinic didn't open until nine. If that was the case, she'd have to run a few errands first and come back later.

But maybe she'd be in luck and one of Rick's office staff would be here. It wouldn't hurt to find out.

So after opening the rear passenger door and removing the clothes hanger from the hook, she locked the car and carried the shirt to the main entrance.

The door was open, so she let herself into the waiting room, which was just as empty as the parking lot.

She stood there for a moment, then raised her voice and asked, "Is anyone here?"

"I am," Rick called out. "I'll be right with you."

And there went her wacky pulse rate again.

Several escalated heartbeats later, Rick entered the waiting room wearing a pair of jeans, a chambray shirt with the sleeves rolled up and a crooked grin.

Rather than let the awkwardness set in, as it was

prone to do whenever they were alone, she handed him the shirt on the hanger. "Here you go. As good as new."

"Amazing," he said, as he looked it over. Then he flashed her a smile that lit his eyes to a mesmerizing shade of blue. "Do you hire out? I've been looking for a new laundry service."

Oh, good. A joke. That she could handle.

She crossed her arms and returned his smile. "Sorry. I might have considered it, but I just received word that I got the social worker position at the medical center. So I'll only have time to wash and iron my own things from now on."

"You got the job? That's great, Mal." He reached out and placed his hand on her shoulder, giving it a gentle squeeze.

It was a friendly gesture—a congratulatory motion any old friend might make. Yet his mere touch sent a spiral of heat to her core.

And a stab of guilt to her chest.

"Thanks," she said, nodding toward the door. "I… uh, really need to go. My grandfather is being released from the hospital today, and I'm taking him to his apartment. I also need to meet with the in-home health care staff who will be with him there. Then I have a meeting with the HR department at the medical center. Needless to say, there's a lot to do before Lucas gets home from school."

"Okay. Give your grandfather my best."

His comment gave her pause. It was a nice thing for him to say, yet offering his thoughtful regard set off a slew of apprehension in her.

But why was that? Surely Grandpa would accept Rick's well wishes with grace.

"I'll tell him," she said. "Thank you."

"Maybe Lucas and I should take you out to dinner this evening—or one night this week to celebrate your new job—and your grandfather's recovery."

The apprehension she'd felt earlier, as well as the heat from his touch, rose up into a fiery ball in her throat, making it nearly impossible to think, let alone speak.

But there was no way she could go out to dinner with Rick.

"That would be nice," she said, "but I'm going to be so busy getting ready and organized for the days and weeks ahead, that I'd rather not make any plans."

He cocked his head slightly, as if challenging her excuse. But it made perfect sense to her. Well, maybe not perfect, but it was at least passable.

"With the new job and finding quality time for Lucas and my grandfather," she added, "well, I'm sure you understand."

His smile faded, and he took a step back. "Of course. Maybe another time."

"Sure."

She nodded toward the clinic door. "I'd better go. I don't want to keep Grandpa waiting."

Rick didn't respond. He just stood there, his gaze locked on hers as if he'd heard all she'd been thinking and very little of what she'd actually said.

But she didn't dare explain herself or drag out the conversation any longer. She had to leave—and quickly, before his receptionist came to work. And before the waiting room filled with pet owners.

All Mallory needed was for everyone in town to think that she and Rick were a couple, especially with Brian arriving next Monday.

As she turned to go, Rick stopped her. "You know what tomorrow is, don't you?"

She stopped at the doorway, her hand on the knob. Then she slowly turned around. "Yes, it's Tuesday."

"I told you I'd give you a week to tell Lucas I was his father. Have you done it yet?"

Her heart dropped to the pit of her stomach. "No, I haven't. But I plan to. I really do. Can you please give me a couple more days? I'd like for him to settle in at the new school."

Rick merely stared at her. Did he think she was trying to put him off indefinitely?

"Lucas deserves to know the truth," she said. "And the sooner the better. But since I'm the one who misled him, I'd like to be the one to set him straight."

"Misled him?" Rick said. "You lied to him."

"Yes, I did. And I'll correct that within the week."

Doubt—or maybe disappointment—clouded his gaze. But she wouldn't worry about that now. She *couldn't.*

"I have to go, Rick. I have a lot to do today. But I'll call you as soon as I've told Lucas the truth."

Then she turned to the door. As she let herself out, she could feel him watching her every step of the way.

Mallory might have made mistakes in the past, but she was doing her best to create a brand-new future for her and Lucas in Brighton Valley. And that future was about to get under way.

Hopefully she'd be so caught up with her new job and in being a devoted and loving granddaughter and mother that she'd be too busy to give the past any thought at all.

Now if she could just rid herself of the memory of Rick's gaze, his scent and his touch, then her life would be back on track.

Chapter Seven

As Rick watched Mallory leave the clinic, he wondered if he should have refused to give her the extra time to tell Lucas—not that he'd actually come out and agreed. But once the secret was out, the two of them would be facing each other on a regular basis, and then where would that leave him?

Just look where his dinner suggestion had gotten him.

What in the hell had he been thinking? Of course she wouldn't want to celebrate with him. Yet for some dumb reason, he'd asked her, anyway, and the question had just popped out the way his invitation to the Lazaros' house had done last week.

Sure, he still felt a powerful attraction to her. And he knew she felt it, too. But she'd torn the heart out of him once upon a time, and he wasn't about to let her do it again.

She'd passed on his dinner suggestion, which was just as well. Rick had things to do, too. He'd been planning to open up his practice to both large and small animals, which meant he would have to find another vet to work with him. The time hadn't been right when he'd first taken over for Doc Grimes, but things had really picked up lately.

So he'd would stick to his original plan to avoid Mallory for a while, which ought to be easy. With Lucas in school now, he wouldn't be springing any surprise visits at the clinic. And Mallory would be tied up with her new job and her obligations to her grandfather.

All Rick had to do was mind his own business, and the distance he wanted to create wouldn't take any effort on his part. In fact, it would happen as naturally as a rooster's crow at sunrise.

But on Wednesday afternoon, at a quarter to four, Rick learned that when kids were involved, nature didn't always run a predictable course.

He'd just left the rescue yard, where he'd taken a lab-mix named Roscoe to the dog run next to Buddy's, when Kara met him at the back door of the clinic.

"Dr. Martinez? Mallory Dickinson is on the phone. She'd like to speak to you."

He couldn't imagine why. "Thanks, Kara. I'll take the call in my office."

Rick stopped by the sink and washed his hands, then he proceeded to the telephone on his desk. Once he settled into his seat, he pushed the lighted button indicating which line was on hold.

"Hey, Mallory. What's up?"

"I'm sorry to bother you, but there's a problem with Lucas, and I thought… Well…"

Rick sat up straight. "What's wrong? Is he okay?"

"Oh, he's not hurt or sick. But I just got back from meeting with the principal and with Mrs. Privett, his teacher. Apparently he was involved in a fight."

"Already? He's only been in school three days. What happened?"

"I wish I knew, but he refuses to give us any details. He has a split lip and a puffy eye—not exactly a shiner, but someone definitely hit him."

"And it happened at school?"

"Yes, and from what we've been able to piece together, it happened outside the classroom, at the end of the day and after the last bell rang. I asked him about it when he got into the car, but he wouldn't say a word. So I parked and took him into the principal's office."

Rick wasn't so sure that was the approach she should have taken, but maybe that's because he'd found himself in the hot seat in a principal's office too many times in the past. But what did he know about disciplining a child?

"Lucas wouldn't tell any of us what happened, either. I have reason to believe there's a bully at school, but I can't very well accuse someone if I don't have any proof."

No, she couldn't do that, but Rick hated the idea of anyone picking on his son.

Would it be wrong to give Lucas some pointers on how to throw a few punches, at least to defend himself?

"Would you mind coming over to talk to him?" Mallory asked. "Maybe he'll be more forthcoming with a man."

Mallory, a trained social worker, was asking Rick's advice on how to parent?

His first thought was that he'd better go to the library or to the bookstore for some self-help books on raising kids. But he didn't have time for that. So he'd have to wing it—as awkward as that might be.

He'd looked forward to being a father when it came to taking Lucas fishing and going to sporting events, like football and baseball. But he hadn't planned on cracking the whip or laying down rules.

Still, Mallory wanted his help, and he couldn't let her down.

"I'll stop by after office hours." He glanced at the patient schedule Kara had posted for him. "How about five-thirty?"

"That's fine. We'll be here."

Rick might not have any experience to draw on, but somehow he'd try to find the right words to say.

Besides, Mallory hadn't asked him to step up and be a father. She'd only asked him to talk to Lucas— man to boy.

How hard could that be?

When Rick arrived at Mallory's house, she met him outside.

"Thanks for coming," she said. "He's not happy that I called you, but I felt a little out of my element."

Good, that made two of them.

The deadline for his ultimatum had come and gone yesterday, and Rick was glad he'd decided not to force the issue just yet. He'd come to realize that he'd needed some time to adjust to the whole idea of fatherhood, too.

And right now, in all honesty, he was glad that he was wearing the hat of a family friend.

When Mallory invited Rick into her living room,

he chose a seat on the sofa, across from Lucas, who sat rather stoically in the easy chair, his arms folded.

Just as she'd said, the boy didn't appear too happy about the upcoming interrogation.

Rick couldn't say that he blamed him. He remembered what it had felt like to be nine years old and questioned about one of the fights he'd been involved in. He also tried to imagine what Hank might have said to him, had Hank been his father—instead of the old man he'd had.

When nothing especially fatherly or pithy came immediately to mind, he opened the conversation by making a lighthearted observation. "Looks like you're going to have an impressive shiner."

Rick stole a glance at Mallory, whose brow shot up. Clearly he'd crossed some line he should have known about.

Strike one.

Rick focused on Lucas. Damn if the boy didn't look like Joey right now, especially with that battered face and stubborn expression.

"So how does the other guy look?" Rick asked, this time avoiding Mallory's gaze completely.

At that, Lucas finally turned to Rick, his lips quirking into the slightest of smiles. "About like me, I guess. But a little worse. He got a bloody nose."

So at least he'd admitted to being involved in a fight.

"It's tough when kids pick on the new guy at school," Rick said.

"Nobody picked on me," Lucas said. "And after today, I don't think they will."

Mallory's breath caught, although Rick didn't think Lucas had noticed.

Was she concerned that Lucas may have picked a fight to show how tough he was? Or was she worried that he might have inherited a propensity for violence, thanks to the Martinez gene pool?

Maybe she just didn't like Rick's line of questioning. But if that was the case, she'd asked for his help. And, for better or worse, she was getting the best he had to offer.

"So what did you do?" Rick asked his son. "Walk up to the biggest guy at school and let him have it?"

"I don't want to talk about it. I might get someone else in trouble, and I'd rather spend all of fourth grade in detention and the rest of my life stuck in my bedroom without any TV."

That was rather noble of him. Rick risked another peek at Mallory, saw her furrow her brow. Then she eased forward, knelt beside the easy chair where Lucas sat and placed her hand on his knee. "You won't be punished for telling the truth, Lucas. No matter what you do, even if it's wrong or bad, if you come to me and tell me about it, I'll support you in every way I can. And if there's someone who needs protection, I want you to share that with me, too. But I can't help you or anyone else if I don't know what's going on."

Lucas dropped his gaze. He seemed to think about what she'd said for the longest time. When he looked up, he bit down on his swollen lip, then winced.

Finally, his gaze met his mother's. "You promise not to say anything to anyone? Hope to die and flash a zillion laser beams in your eye?"

Apparently, the cost to secret-breakers had gone up with the rise in technology.

"I promise," she said. "But if someone's in danger,

we'll have to discuss ways you can best help them. And sometimes that will be by telling the right people."

Lucas seemed to consider the maternal wisdom, then he turned to Rick. "Doctors have to keep secrets when their patients tell them stuff. So that means you can't tell, either, right?"

The boy was getting his professional ethics a bit mixed up, especially when it came to veterinarians, but that wasn't the point right now. And as long as Mallory was handling the danger-to-others scenario, Rick was in the clear. So he raised his right hand in Boy Scout fashion. "I promise."

The boy nodded solemnly, as if they'd made a sacred vow. The three of them.

A family pact.

Finally, Lucas began to open up. "Do you know how bad it is to be a foster kid?" he asked.

Now it was Rick's turn to raise his brow and glance at Mallory. When he looked back at Lucas, he said, "Yeah, I actually *do* know. And while there are plenty of good homes out there, that's not always the case. And the bad ones can really suck."

"Well, when you're a kid who's lived in some of those bad families and have to move around a lot, it's really hard. So when you finally find a home that's a good one, and you got a foster dad you really like, you can't get into any trouble. 'Cause if you do, you could get kicked out. Or then they can take you to another foster home—one of the bad ones."

Rick wasn't sure where Lucas was going with this, but he suspected that Ryan and Jason were involved.

"So let me see if I've got this straight," Rick said.

"You got into a fight today, trying to protect a kid who's afraid he'll get kicked out of a good home?"

"Kind of," Lucas said. "You see, there's this cool second grader at my school who was getting picked on all the time by this big jerk bully in the fourth grade. And the kid's older brother wanted to stand up for him. But he was afraid to get in a fight and kick the bully's butt because he could have got into big trouble."

"So, as a favor to the brothers, you fought the bully?" Mallory asked.

Lucas nodded. "And that's why I can't tell anyone about it. And since the big jerk bully got his butt kicked, he's not going to pick on me or my friends anymore."

Mallory probably wouldn't agree, but Rick was proud of his son. Not that he wanted Lucas to get into fights—or to be a troublemaker in school—but the boy was loyal and brave. Who could fault him for that?

So now what?

Rick's old man—and his uncle, too—would have ignored the whole thing as no big deal and never would have had a sit-down talk with him at all. That is, unless the school contacted them. And even then, they would have blown the whole thing off as an inconvenience.

But no way did Rick want to follow their lead. Instead, he wondered how Hank would have handled the situation.

He supposed, knowing his mentor as he did, that Hank would have addressed the heart of the matter. And that's what Rick would try to do. So he leaned forward and rested his forearms on his knees. "Did you know that Jason and Ryan, the boys who live at Tom Randall's ranch, are foster kids?"

Lucas studied him. His brows raised slightly, but he didn't respond.

"I'm going to take a big leap here," Rick said. "I'm going to assume that you're talking about those boys. And that a kid at your school has been making trouble for them."

Lucas started to bite down on his swollen lip again, but caught himself.

"I was a foster kid, too," Rick said. "And I didn't grow up in loving homes. Not like the ones you've had—or the one Jason and Ryan now have with Tom. So I know how boys like them think. They're scared and unsettled most of the time. They've learned at a young age that they can't trust the adults in their lives. And when they finally get a good home and meet people like Tom Randall, they're afraid to go to them and tell them when they're scared or in some kind of trouble."

"Like I was afraid to talk to my mom and to you today?" Lucas asked.

"Exactly. You didn't trust us, even though the adults in your life have been good to you. When you were hungry, they fed you. And when you were hurt, they comforted you. But Jason and Ryan haven't always lived with people who loved and cared for them. So a lot of the time, they had to deal with their fears and problems on their own."

"That's really sad," Lucas said.

"Well, yes. It used to be. But things are much better now. Jason and Ryan don't know this yet, but one day they will. Tom Randall is one of the nicest and kindest men I know. He's got a good heart. That's why he took those boys to live with him on his ranch in the first place. So believe me, they can trust him when they're hungry or hurt—and when they're scared or in trouble. If they would have told him about the bully, he would have given them good advice. In fact, tomorrow, when you see them at school, I hope you'll tell them what I just said."

At that, Mallory stepped in. "Rick's right, Lucas. And even if the boys had gotten into a fight—and into trouble—Tom wouldn't have sent them away. Everyone makes mistakes, and Tom is there to help Jason and Ryan learn from theirs so that they can make better choices the next time."

Lucas sat there for the longest time. Then he looked at Rick. "You think that's true? Their new foster dad wouldn't have kicked them out for getting into a fight?"

"Not even if they'd been the ones to start the fight," Rick said. "I told you that Tom is a friend of mine and that he's a good man. But that's something those boys will have to learn with time. Hopefully, when it comes to trusting the adults in your life, you'll be able to learn that lesson a lot faster. Your mom and I…" Rick caught himself and paused.

He saw Mallory watching him, no doubt afraid he'd spill the beans, but he'd promised her he wouldn't until she'd given him the okay. He'd tried to force her hand by giving her a time limit, but Lucas had enough to deal with today. In fact, they all had. So he chose his words carefully and followed through on the comment he'd stalled on just a couple of beats before.

"Your mom is always going to be there for you, Lucas. And you have my phone number. You also know where I live and work. If you ever need a friend, all you have to do is say the word. The door to my house and my clinic is always open to you."

"That's pretty cool, Dr. Martinez."

Yeah, well, it was the best he could do until Mallory told their son who he really was.

Hell, it might be the best he could do, anyway. Still, Rick wanted Lucas to know the truth. And he didn't want to prolong things much longer.

"You know," Rick added, "I used to get into trouble a lot when I was in school—usually for fighting. And sometimes for other things I'd rather not admit to. So I spent my share of time in the principal's office and in detention."

"Did you get sent to your room, too?" Lucas asked.

Sent to his room? No, Rick usually got knocked across it, which was why he'd learned to stay away from the house whenever he had reason to believe his dad or his uncle were in a mood that could easily turn volatile.

"Yeah, I got punished," he admitted. "But I was so angry and stubborn that it didn't seem to help much. In fact, I grew up with a real chip on my shoulder."

"Who were you mad at?" the boy asked.

"The world, it seemed."

"What happened to make you stop?" Lucas asked.

I met your mom, Rick thought about saying. But in all honesty, after he and Mallory split, Rick had ended up in a worse place than when she'd found him.

"One day I ran into Hank Lazaro," Rick said. "He's the guy who had the barbecue at his house last Saturday. And just like Tom Randall stepped up and offered a home and the promise of a new future to Jason and Ryan, Hank did the same thing for me."

"You mean Mr. Lazaro was your foster dad?"

"No, I was practically grown up when I met Hank. But I do think of him as a father because he taught me

important things like integrity, respect, self-control, responsibility and the value of a hard day's work." Rick's
gaze drifted from the boy to Mallory, who'd been staring at him.

For a couple of heartbeats there seemed to be some
kind of connection between them, something he could
almost touch. Then she turned to their son.

"So what do you think?" she asked him. "Can you
trust the adults in your life to love you, care for you
and offer sound advice, instead of getting into fights?"

"Yeah," he said. "I guess so."

They sat like that, the three of them. Father. Mother.
Son. They weren't quite a family, but they weren't
strangers, either.

As Rick relished the closeness, as fragile as it
seemed, an idea sparked—something Hank had done
for Rick. Something Rick could do for Lucas.

"You once asked me if you could get a job working
for me at the clinic," Rick said to the boy. "And I was
just thinking that I could probably use you a couple of
days each week—when you get out of school. That is,
if it's okay with your mom."

Lucas brightened. "No kidding? That would be
really cool."

"Don't get too excited," Rick said. "There's one con-
dition—a big one. You'd have to prove to your mom
and me that you're responsible. And you do that by
doing three things, all of which you'd have to do before you can even ask your mom for her permission to
work for me."

"What's that?" Lucas asked.

"You have to obey your mother at home and your

teacher at school. And that means you'd have to do your chores, get your homework done and stay out of fights."

"I can do that," Lucas said.

Rick risked a glance at Mallory, whose eyes were watery. Rick didn't know if that was a good thing or not. But when Mallory sent Lucas upstairs, he figured he'd find out soon enough.

The boy got to his feet, but instead of going to his room, he padded over to the sofa, where Rick sat. Then he bent over and gave him a hug.

The embrace had been so unexpected, so heartfelt, that Rick wasn't quite sure how to respond at first. So he wrapped his arms loosely around the boy and patted him on the back.

Next Lucas hugged Mallory, only this time, the boy fell into her embrace, and she seemed to know just what to do, how tight to squeeze and how long to hold him close.

Moments later, Lucas headed up the stairs, leaving the adults alone. Mallory got to her feet, and Rick followed her lead.

"I can't tell you how much I appreciate you coming over to talk to him," she said, her eyes still misty. "It's not easy relating to a growing boy, especially when handling all the day-to-day stuff is still so new to me."

"Thanks for calling me. I have to admit, this sort of thing is a little out of my league, but I tried to remember what it was like to be his age. And to imagine what Hank might have said to me."

"Well, your instincts were spot on. And everything you said to him was perfect." She reached out her hand, although he wasn't sure why.

In appreciation? As a way of extending some sort of parental olive branch?

Or was she giving him another hint that it was time for him to go?

Either way, he took her hand in his. But the moment they touched, a jolt of heat shot right through him.

When their gazes locked, her pretty green eyes widened, and her lips parted, letting him know that she'd felt the powerful jolt, too.

For a moment, they were teenagers again, walking to the back of the library, where their feelings were so tender, so innocent, so sweet....

So undeniably strong.

He placed his left hand along her jaw and caressed her cheek with his thumb. Kissing her seemed like the most natural thing in the world to do right now. And while the guy he used to be might have considered doing just that, the man he'd become didn't take something that didn't belong to him.

And as much as he'd begun to wish otherwise, Mallory belonged to someone else.

Before he could withdraw his hand, she took a step back and said, "It's time, Rick. I'm ready."

He cocked his head slightly, unsure of what she meant and afraid to make any false assumptions. "Ready for what?"

"To level with Lucas. He needs to know the truth about you. Today's been pretty emotional for all of us, so I'd rather wait until tomorrow. But when I sit down with him, I'd like you to be here."

"All right. Same time tomorrow afternoon?"

She nodded.

Okay. Rick could do that.

But something told him stealing a kiss today and risking her rejection might have been easier than what he would have to face tomorrow after Lucas learned the truth.

Because things were getting more and more complicated between him and his son's mother with each passing day.

Rick might have denied Marie's words earlier, but there was no denying them now. Whatever he and Mallory had felt for each other before still burned bright, even if one or the other might claim otherwise.

But he couldn't see how that was going to change anything in the long run. It certainly hadn't mattered ten years ago.

And like before, a child still hung in the balance.

Chapter Eight

The next twenty-four hours passed agonizingly slow for Mallory as she pondered what she would say to her son.

At one time she'd worried about the kind of father Rick would be—or if he'd even want to take on a parental role. But he'd stepped right up to the plate yesterday and had given their son some excellent advice.

Lucas must have taken Rick's words to heart. At least, he'd seemed to. And by the time she'd picked him up at school, the trouble with the bully seemed to have been resolved.

She'd arrived early and had been tempted to walk to the classroom and escort him to the car, just to make sure there weren't any more end-of-the-day scuffles. But she hadn't wanted anyone to think that she was a helicopter mom, so she'd forced herself to wait patiently in the vehicle line with the other parents.

After Lucas had climbed into the passenger seat, she'd tossed him a smile and asked, "How'd it go today?"

"It was okay. But me and Dylan had to go to the office to talk to the principal."

Dylan Jessup was the boy she'd suspected he'd fought with yesterday. "Why did the principal want to see you? Did you tell her that Dylan was the other boy involved in the fight?"

"I didn't have to. When Dylan's teacher saw his black eye this morning, she must have told on him."

"Did you both admit to fighting?" she asked.

"Dylan didn't, but I told Mrs. Privett that he was picking on my friend for a long time. And that when I told him to stop, he told me to shut up and pushed me away. So we got in a fight."

"Then what happened?"

"Me and Dylan have to go to detention for five days, starting tomorrow. There's a note in my backpack. I'll show it to you when we get home."

"Did Dylan have anything to say about the punishment?"

"No. I think he likes detention."

"He does?"

"Why else would he keep getting in trouble?"

Mallory had smiled at his simple logic, then she'd asked about Jason and Ryan.

"Dylan didn't mess with them today."

"I'm glad to hear that. Did you tell them what Dr. Martinez said?"

"Yeah. I'm not sure if they're going to talk to their foster dad about being scared he might kick them out. But they might."

That was a step in the right direction, she supposed.

When they arrived at home, Mallory gave Lucas a snack, then had him do his homework, which was a page of math and a section in his social studies workbook. Afterward she let him play a video game in the den while she waited for Rick to arrive.

She glanced at her wristwatch. Rick was a couple of minutes late, although she knew there had to be a good reason for it. But that didn't make her any less nervous, any less eager to get her confession over with.

Just thinking about having to admit her dishonesty had kept her up late last night. And it had her pacing the living room floor now.

She'd felt this same way ten years ago, when she'd been seventeen, unwed and pregnant.

Knowing how badly she was going to hurt and disappoint her grandparents had made her want to hide in her room and never come out. But she'd finally had no choice but to tell them. Then she'd watched their pained expressions, the shock, the disappointment.

Telling them, hurting them, watching her grandmother cry, had been the hardest thing she'd ever had to do. At least, up until that day.

The next hardest thing had been leaving Rick. But she hadn't been able to stay in Brighton Valley. She'd had to leave before her pregnancy began to show, before she embarrassed her grandparents. So she'd gone to Boston, where she was to stay until after she'd given up the baby.

And that had been the very hardest thing of all.

Once at her aunt's house, she'd cried every night for the baby she'd yet to meet, the child who'd been conceived in love and who would be given up in the very same manner.

When she'd heard about open adoptions, she'd realized that was the only way she could possibly live with her decision. She'd be able to please her grandparents, continue her education and provide a baby for a childless couple without losing her son completely.

However, when she'd broached the idea with Rick, he'd refused to even consider what had been a perfect solution for her. Instead, he'd signed the paperwork, giving up all parental rights.

She'd been crushed. Hurt. And she'd never felt so alone in her life.

A knock sounded, drawing her from the melancholy musing, and she blew out a sigh before answering.

Rick entered the living room wearing a pair of worn jeans and a black T-shirt and looking so much like the adult version of the teenager rebel she'd once loved.

"I'm sorry I'm late," he said, "but I had an emergency surgery this afternoon and couldn't leave until the dog was out of recovery."

"That's okay. I knew you'd be here when you could." She tucked a strand of hair behind her ear, wishing she could tuck away her scattered emotions just as easily.

Would she ever get used to seeing Rick again, to having him in her house and in her life?

She stepped aside, allowing him further entrance. But as she did so, he not only filled the living room with his musky scent, but his raw, masculine essence set off every atom and ion in the air, jumpstarting all the memories she had of the two of them and threatening to resurrect her old feelings for him.

But she tamped it all down nearly as soon as it rose up.

"Where's Lucas?" Rick asked.

"Upstairs. I'll call him down." Better yet, maybe she'd better go up and get him. She could use a couple of minutes to gather her thoughts.

And then, after today, after she confessed to Lucas and the resulting conversation was behind her, she would take some time away from the local vet to let the dust—and the memories—settle.

Brian would be flying in on Monday, and they had a commitment, an understanding. He was making a huge move halfway across the country for her—and he'd been so kind, so patient.

She was tempted to call Brian and tell him that she needed more time before he came out to visit, but she couldn't very well do that. She'd made the poor man wait long enough as it was. Even his family, at least his brother, was beginning to ask him what he saw in her. And one of these days he was going to question that himself—if he hadn't already.

Yet even with the couple of minutes it took to go after Lucas, especially after listening to him complain about pausing the game when he was just about to reach an especially high level of Utopia, she didn't feel any better about what she was about to tell him.

Still, he followed her downstairs.

When Lucas spotted Rick, his footsteps slowed. "Uh-oh. Did something happen to Buddy?"

"No," Rick said. "He's fine."

Lucas looked at Mallory, then back to Rick. "What's everyone frowning about? Am I in trouble again?"

"No," Mallory said. "This time I'm the one who

made a mistake. And I asked Dr. Martinez to be here when I told you about it."

Lucas scrunched his face, his left eye still puffy and a bit discolored from yesterday's playground scuffle. "What did you do?"

"When you were younger, you asked me a question, and I was afraid to tell you the truth. So I didn't. And I need to set things straight now."

The furrow in his brow deepened, reminding her of her grandfather. And while it was nice to see that he'd actually inherited some traits from the Dickinson side of the family, she pressed on with her confession.

"You asked me about your biological father. You wanted me to help you find him, and I told you that he died before you were born."

"You mean he's *not* dead?" Disbelief chased the confusion from his face.

"Let's sit down," Mallory said, gesturing for them all to take a seat.

Lucas ambled toward the easy chair, which he'd taken yesterday, and plopped down. Rick chose the sofa, and she joined him, sitting just a cushion away.

"When I moved to Boston," Mallory began, "I lost touch with your father. And I never expected to see him again. Our breakup wasn't easy on either of us, and there were some hard feelings. To be honest, I thought he'd probably left Brighton Valley a long time ago. He'd moved around a lot when he was younger, and I'd heard his brother had already left town."

Lucas crossed his arms. "You were so mad at him that you didn't even want to look for him? So you told me that he died?"

In a nutshell? Lucas had cut to the heart of the matter, but there'd been other considerations, although they didn't seem to matter that much right now.

"Yes," she said, "I was angry with him. But it's more complicated than that. Still, you need to understand something else. I loved your father very much. But we were both young back then, and we weren't able to give you the kind of home and family you deserved."

"You told me that before."

Mallory glanced at Rick, saw him watching her, waiting, allowing her to do the talking, to give her reasons. And while she might have come up with an excuse or two to absolve her guilt in the past, she couldn't seem to find one that worked any longer, especially since throwing Rick under the bus was no longer an option.

"Your father offered to quit school and marry me," she said. "But I knew he would need an education to get the kind of job that would support a wife and family, especially if I wanted to attend college, too."

"So you told him no," Lucas said. "And then you gave me away and let the Dunlops adopt me."

He'd never accused her of "giving him away" before, and the words sliced into her now. But she suspected that he'd meant them to hurt.

Or maybe the decision she'd made back then had left her so raw, so vulnerable, that anything he might have said would have torn her wide-open.

Either way, the story wasn't new to him. Sue and Gary had always told him he'd been chosen, special. And that's the part she would cling to now.

"I knew that Sue and Gary would love you with all their hearts," Mallory said. "They owned their own home, they had stable jobs and they were able to give you all the things that your father and I wanted you to have."

"Okay," Lucas said. "I get that. But if my dad isn't dead, then where is he?"

Mallory glanced at Rick, then back at Lucas. "I didn't realize this since I hadn't talked to him in more than nine years, but your father isn't the same guy I once knew. He went to college and became a respected member of the community."

"So when do I get to meet him?" Lucas asked.

"You already have."

Lucas shot a glance at Rick, but didn't crack a smile. "*You're* my dad? And that's why I look like you?"

Rick nodded. "Yes."

"And you guys didn't tell me until now?" The boy chuffed, then crossed his arms.

"Don't blame Rick for that," Mallory said. "The minute he saw you, he knew you were his son. He wanted me to tell you right away, but I wasn't ready. I felt badly about lying to you, but at the time you'd asked me about him, Gary had just died. You were a lot younger then, and I didn't think you were ready to meet the Rick I used to know. But after meeting Rick again and realizing how wrong I'd been about him, I didn't know how to go about correcting my mistake."

"When is a lie ever a good idea?" Lucas asked, sounding a whole lot like Gary Dunlop right now.

As if sensing that Mallory was at a complete loss, Rick stepped in. "Your mom is one of the most honest people I've ever known, Lucas. She lied to you to protect me."

Lucas scrunched his face.

"Let me explain." Rick leaned forward and placed

his forearms on his knees. "One of the reasons your mom and I lost touch with each other is because I was opposed to the idea of an open adoption."

At that, Lucas appeared more hurt than angry. "You were? How come?"

"I thought it would be too hard on me. How was I supposed to be a part of your life when I lived so far away from you? I'd never get to see you. Besides that, I was young and didn't know how to be a father. My dad hadn't been a good example. And I also thought that Gary Dunlop would be a much better dad than I could ever be."

Lucas seemed to ponder that for a while. As he did, silence filled the room until Mallory thought she ought to rise up and say something, although she wasn't sure what.

Finally Lucas turned to her. "I can't believe you lied to me, though. My other mom and dad *never* lied."

Guilt rose up and jabbed her in the chest, shoving her back, making her feel as though she'd not only failed her son, but that she'd failed Gary and Sue, too.

"Don't be too hard on your mom," Rick said. "She did what she thought was best back then. And she's trying to come clean now. In fact, we both are."

"It's not that I don't like you," Lucas said, "but I think this whole thing sucks."

So did Mallory, but there wasn't much she could do about it now, other than to apologize.

"I'm sorry, Lucas. I was wrong. I should have told you the truth. All I can do is promise never to lie to you again. Will you please forgive me?"

Lucas didn't answer right away. About the time she

thought he might hold it against her indefinitely, he said, "I guess so."

"Will you forgive me, too?" Rick asked. "Sometimes we make decisions when we're young and dumb, and they're not always the best ones. Luckily, your mom and I have a second chance to get things right. And even though you and I are getting a late start, I want you to know that I'm glad you're my son. And that I'd like to be a part of your life, even if it's just as a friend and mentor—like Hank Lazaro is to me."

Mallory couldn't imagine how Lucas could say no to that. The kid was such a loving child. Sue and Gary had done wonders with him, even though he could be a bit rebellious and stubborn at times.

"Remember what you said to me yesterday?" Lucas asked Rick. "You talked about adults not doing what they're supposed to do and kids not trusting them."

Mallory glanced at Rick, their gazes communicating in a way they hadn't done in years. *He's a smart kid. Parenting him isn't going to be easy.*

"Point taken," Rick told the boy. "But in time, you're going to realize that you *can* trust your mom and me to be honest and to do right by you from now on."

"I hope so," Lucas said. Then he turned to Mallory. "Can I go back to the den now and finish playing my video game?"

"Sure." Mallory waited until he'd gone upstairs and his bedroom door closed to blow out the breath she'd been holding. But she hadn't been able to hold back the tears that welled in her eyes.

Mallory turned to Rick, her bottom lip quivering, a tear slipping down her cheek. He was tempted to take her in his arms and hold her close, just as he had when she'd come to him in tears ten years ago, scared to death of what her grandfather was going to say when she told him that she was pregnant.

"I think you're safe," Rick had told her back then. "I'm probably the one who'll be facing the wrong end of his shotgun."

The minister hadn't turned violent, like some of Rick's family had been prone to do, but he'd still hit the roof and had threatened to have Rick arrested for statutory rape.

Rick hadn't believed the courts would see it that way, especially since he'd just turned eighteen and had been willing to marry Mallory, but she'd disagreed. Her grandfather had been prominent in the community and knew people. In fact, the D.A. was a golf buddy of his. So she'd gone along with his wishes to leave town, give the baby away and then return with no one the wiser.

She hadn't come back, though. And the rest was history.

In fact, so much history had taken place since she'd left town ten years ago that an embrace, no matter how tempting, was no longer appropriate.

"Thanks for telling Lucas not to blame me," she said.

"Yeah, well I'm not sure there are any real villains in this scenario," he said. Not even her grandfather, although Rick had always thought of him as one.

Maybe he ought to stop by and visit the retired minister one of these days. That might go a long way in mending fences.

Rick and Mallory continued to sit on the sofa, not quite close enough to touch, yet still connected in ways neither of them could deny any longer.

"I did love you," she said.

He'd loved her, too. But he wasn't going to admit it. Not when they'd just promised Lucas they'd be honest with each other from this day forward. Because a confession like that might lead to a truth he was just beginning to wrap his heart and mind around—he'd probably never stopped loving her at all.

"But back then," Mallory added, "we really weren't in a position to get married and provide a home for Lucas."

"You're right. I realize that now."

They drifted back into silence, neither of them moving. Instead, they seemed to be lost in their thoughts, their memories—and maybe even their regrets.

"After you left, I waited for your calls," he said, "but they were so few and far between that it felt as though you'd pretty much shut me out of your life."

"My aunt Carrie wanted me to cut all ties with you, and while I hated being so far away and not keeping in closer contact, I tried to respect her wishes. I figured I'd gotten into enough trouble as it was, and…"

He finished her sentence for her. "And you wanted to prove to her that you were still a good girl."

"I guess you're right." She bit down on her bottom lip. "But not a day went by that I didn't think about you. That I didn't cry myself to sleep."

She'd finally contacted him through a friend when she'd been about eight months pregnant, and he'd thought that she was calling to tell him she'd changed her mind about him, about *them,* about the baby. And for a couple of heartbeats, he hadn't felt so all alone anymore.

Instead, she'd told him she'd found a great couple

who would be perfect parents, although her words had just buzzed in his ears.

She was *really* going to do it, he'd thought. She was going to give away their baby. And Rick had realized that he'd lost his one shot being a part of a real family.

So when she'd told him that she'd wanted an open adoption, where birth parents kept in touch with their kids and the new families, he'd balked. He couldn't even fathom a thing like that. He'd either wanted to be the only father in his kid's life, or he'd wanted to walk away and pretend the whole thing had never happened. As far as he'd been concerned back then, it had to be either all or nothing.

But in truth, there'd been another question he'd asked himself. What kind of dad would he have made? After all, he'd been such a crappy big brother that Joey hadn't even turned to him when things got rough. Instead, he'd run away from home and had disappeared from the planet.

So in his pain, in his disappointment, Rick had told Mallory, *Do whatever you want. I don't want anything to do with the baby or with the adoption plan. Send me the paperwork, and I'll sign off. I'm done.*

He'd thought he heard her voice crack, thought his words had hurt her, but he hadn't cared. She'd hurt him by refusing to marry him, and turnabout had seemed to be fair play.

"I thought you'd call me when the baby was born," he said.

She shot a glance at him, her gaze lancing his. "You told me not to bother."

The truth in her words slammed into him. "I didn't

mean it. I was so hurt, all I could think of was lashing back at you."

"It worked," she said.

Apparently, it had. Because she hadn't come back to Brighton Valley like she'd told him she would. And he supposed that had been his fault, too.

At the time, he'd told himself it hadn't mattered. But it had, because once Mallory was no longer at school, Rick hadn't want to be there, either. He'd dropped out before Thanksgiving.

Thank God Hank Lazaro had come around when he had.

"I'm sorry for hurting you," Rick said. "I can't make up for the pain I caused you in the past. All I can say is that I was young and didn't have anyone to turn to for guidance back then. But I promise to be more considerate in the future."

"Apology accepted. So now what are we going to do?"

"About Lucas?" Or about their youthful romance that had been doomed from the start?

"Yes. He's pretty upset."

"Give him some time. We dumped a lot on him tonight."

"You're right."

Rick hoped so. But he really wasn't sure.

"I guess we'll have to learn how to coparent," she said.

"We seem to be making a pretty good start—for novices."

She turned to him and smiled, her eyes red-rimmed and puffy—yet still as pretty as ever, still as attractive.

So what the hell were they going to do about that

damned youthful romance? She hadn't asked him about that. But the question was due to come up someday because his feelings for Mallory had come back full force.

Still, even though he'd turned his life around, and the past ten years had brought a lot of changes, she was still out of reach.

And now he had a son, a boy who'd once thought he hung the moon—until he learned about the teenager Rick had once been.

All Rick had ever wanted to do was to put the past behind him, but now he feared his mistakes and bad decisions would haunt him the rest of his life.

The next day had been busy, and Rick had to work through lunch. So late that afternoon, he'd finally taken a break and had gone back to his office, where he ate a sandwich at his desk.

He'd no more than taken a second bite when Kara buzzed him to let him know he had a call on line one.

"Who is it?" he asked.

"Your aunt."

"Thanks." He didn't pick up right away. Instead, he thought about having Kara give *Tia* Rosa a reason he couldn't talk now. But he figured she'd just call back later or try and reach him at home tonight. So he put down his sandwich, pushed the lighted button and connected the line.

"Hi, *Tia*. What's going on?"

"Quite a bit, actually. I know you advised against it, but I went out to dinner with your uncle. And it was nice. *He* was nice. I really think the change in him is real. I was wondering if you'd come over to my house to meet with us one night this week."

No way would Rick agree to do that. He didn't want to re-establish a relationship with his uncle—especially if Ramon and Rosa reconciled. He'd fought too long and too hard to shake the shame and embarrassment of the past. And all he needed was for his uncle to backslide and start drinking.

"I'm sorry, *Tia*. I'm tied up this week."

"Then maybe next week."

"Actually, this entire month is going to be tough. I'm interviewing other vets interested in joining my practice, plus I have some personal issues that have cropped up."

"Oh."

He could hear the disappointment in her voice, and while he didn't want to hurt her feelings, he'd finally managed to create a respectable standing in the community, and he didn't need to be associated with a couple prone to drunken brawls that sometimes turned violent and required police intervention.

Rick had Lucas to think about now. And, in a way, he had Mallory, too.

"I know you still love him," Rick said. "But I'm going to level with you, *Tia*. Even if my schedule lightens up, I'm not going to agree to meeting with the two of you. I'm not in support of a reconciliation, so I'm not going to get involved."

"I'm sorry for bothering you," she said.

"You didn't bother me. Feel free to call me anytime. But I've moved on in my life. And dredging up the past isn't something I want to do."

He took a moment to ask about her health and her new job, just so she wouldn't think he was angry. Then they said goodbye.

Still, after the line disconnected, his stomach knotted, and he shoved his sandwich aside.

Maybe he should have been more understanding, but hell, even Joey had taken off for parts unknown, wanting to put it all behind him—including his own brother.

Is that what Joey had done? Gotten a fresh start?

As he was prone to do whenever Joey crossed his mind, Rick tried to think about what had gone wrong—and what he could have done to prevent his kid brother from running away.

Rick probably should have spent more time with him, talked to him about doing his homework and that sort of thing. After all, the kid never had any real parental figure.

But neither had Rick.

After Joey had run off, Rick had gone out looking for him, but it was as if he'd dropped off the face of the earth. Rick's biggest fear, which had grown steadily each year, was that something bad had happened to him—that he'd died or gone to prison.

Rick had gone so far as to hire a private investigator a couple years ago, but the guy hadn't turned up any leads.

How did a teenager just disappear? In this day and age, with all the computer technology going on, you'd think that...

Rick sat back in his chair. Why hadn't he thought of that before? His old buddy, Clay Jenkins, was a computer whiz who owned Zorba the Geek, a successful national franchise, as well as its affiliate, GeekMart Electronics.

If anyone could do a cyber search and find something, it would be Clay.

Rick immediately buzzed Kara, telling her to hold his calls for a while. Then he pulled out his cell phone and dialed Clay.

Several rings later, his friend answered with an upbeat voice. "Hey, Rick. What's up? I haven't heard from you in ages."

"I know. It's been way too long."

Rick didn't take the time to mention that Mallory had come back to town, that she now had custody of Lucas. There was time to update his buddy later. Right now, he was concerned about finding Joey.

"I was hoping you could do me a favor, Clay. It's been ten years, and I still haven't heard from my brother. I keep imagining the worst, and not knowing is really killing me. I'd like some closure. I can't help blaming myself for not visiting him more when he was in that last foster home. If I'd been a better listener, if I'd spent more time with him…"

"You can't beat yourself up for that," Clay said. "You were just a kid yourself. And you had your own troubles."

Rick and Clay had been pretty tight back then, so his friend knew all too well what the Martinez brothers had been going through.

"I thought that you might be able to help me," Rick said.

"I'll do whatever I can. What do you need?"

"I hired a P.I. a couple of years ago, but he didn't turn up anything. I figured, with your computer skills, you might have better luck."

"Sure. Do you have any personal info? Or do you need me to dig it up?"

Rick gave him what he had—name, birth date and social security number.

"Let me see what I can find out, and I'll get back to you."

Rick thanked him, then asked how things were going for him.

"Actually," Clay said, "I might be coming back to Brighton Valley myself. My first store is losing money like crazy, and I know something's wrong. I'm going to find out whether someone's running it into the ground because of incompetency or because they're siphoning funds."

"Why do it yourself?"

"Because that's where it all started. Hank got me a job there, and Ralph Weston, the previous owner, taught me a lot about business and honesty and hard work. I guess you could say that store has sentimental value. And seeing it go down the tubes like that… Well, it's personal."

"I understand completely. And it'll be good to see you."

They chatted a while longer. Clay asked about Hank and Marie, and Rick told him they were doing well. They'd just hung up the phone when Kara buzzed him.

"I see that you're off the line, Dr. Martinez. Do you have a few minutes?"

"Yes."

"Lucas is here. And he'd like to talk to you—if you're not busy."

"Send him in."

Lucas hadn't been happy when he'd learned that Rick was his dad. Maybe having twenty-four hours to think it over had given him a fresh perspective. Maybe he wanted to start things off on a better foot.

Rick certainly hoped so.

When the boy walked into his office, he stopped short of the desk, then bit down on his lip, just as Mallory was prone to do. "I wanted to talk to you, but I can sit in the waiting room until you're done eating."

Rick wrapped his sandwich back up and smiled. "Have a seat. I was just taking a break."

"I've been thinking about stuff," Lucas said, as he pulled out one of the chairs in front of the desk and took a seat. Again, he bit down on his lip

"So what's on your mind?" Rick asked.

Lucas took a deep breath, then slowly let it out as he narrowed his gaze at Rick. "My mom used to love you. Did you love her, too?"

Rick might have downplayed his feelings in the past—even to himself. But he'd promised the kid not to lie to him, and that was a promise he intended to keep. "Yes, I loved her."

"So are you going to ask her to go out with you?"

The question took him aback, especially with the new honesty-at-all-costs policy. But this one was going to be pretty easy to skate around. "Your mother has a boyfriend."

"Doesn't that bother you?"

Yeah, it bothered him. But what was he supposed to do about it?

"As long as she's involved with another man, dating her isn't an option."

"What if she broke up with Brian? Would you take her to dinner or something?"

Would he? That would mean he'd have to consider being a full-time husband and father. Could he do that?

Could he at least try?

Hank and Marie had shown him a side of family life he'd never seen before, the kind of home and marital relationship a husband and wife ought to have, the kind of love parents should have for their child.

But how much did he dare tell his son, especially if honesty came first and foremost?

"Yes, Lucas. I'd ask her out if she wasn't involved with Brian. But I'm not going to chase after a woman who's in love with another man."

Or a woman who didn't want to be caught.

Chapter Nine

Rick had just finished treating his last patient of the day, a three-year-old cocker spaniel with an ear infection, when Kara informed him that Mallory was on the telephone.

He wondered why she would call. Lucas had left on his bike at least twenty minutes ago, so he should have gotten home already.

"Thanks, Kara. Tell her I'll be with her in a minute."

Ever since Mallory had moved back to town, Rick was finding it harder and harder to get through the day without one interruption or another. And while he didn't mind, he wasn't used to having his receptionist being privy to his personal life, although Kara was discreet. Luckily, she'd also been pretty cool about the whole thing.

He supposed he'd better get used to the interruptions. Something told him he'd be getting more calls when their son hit his teen years.

Rick made his way to the phone in the hallway, just outside the exam rooms. "Hi, Mal. What's up?"

"Buddy's loose again. He must have followed Lucas home."

Rick didn't know how that could have happened. He'd hired a guy to rebuild Buddy's pen so that the energetic pup couldn't jump over it. He'd even had the bottom reinforced so he couldn't dig his way out.

"He ran into the house as soon as Lucas opened the front door," Mallory said. "Can you come and get him?"

"I'm just about finished here, so I can be there in about ten minutes."

After Rick hung up the phone, he continued to rest his hand on the receiver. How had the dog escaped? Had Lucas gone around to the back of the clinic and visited Buddy without Rick's knowledge or permission? Had he opened the gate for some reason?

That was the only logical explanation Rick could come up with. Lucas must have accidentally let the dog out.

Surely he wouldn't have done it intentionally.

Either way, Rick would have to talk to him about it when he got to Mallory's. He couldn't risk having his rescue animals get loose. No telling what could happen to them, especially to Buddy, who didn't have any street smarts.

After he reviewed a lab test, he called the worried owner of a six-year-old Siamese and let her know the infection had cleared up completely. Next he took care of a couple of other things that needed his attention before asking Kara to close the clinic and lock up for the day. Then he went to Mallory's, arriving at her house shortly after he told her he would.

When she answered the door wearing a low-cut pair of stylish black slacks that hugged her curves and a fitted white blouse, she nearly took his breath away. But then again, hadn't that always been the case?

Today she'd swept her hair into a stylish twist, a silver clip holding it in place. She'd carefully applied her makeup, the mascara enhancing those pretty green eyes, the lipstick a kissable shade of pink.

As he studied her, he inhaled her soft floral scent. Before he knew it, he became so caught up in her essence, in how great she looked, in how glad he was to be near her again, that it took him a moment to remember why he was even here.

"Come on in." She stepped aside.

"You look nice," he said. "Did you start work already?"

"Thanks. I don't start until a week from Monday, but I had a meeting with my supervisor earlier this afternoon."

He followed her through the living room, watching the sway of her hips, listening to the click of her heels on the hardwood floor.

"Buddy and Lucas are in the backyard," she said, pointing out the sliding door. "Did you bring a leash?"

"I have it right here." He pulled it out of his back hip pocket.

When he dangled it from his hand, she tossed him a dazzling smile that reached her eyes. He could have gazed at the teenage Mallory all day long, but the grown-up version?

It made a guy wish he could live the past ten years all over again.

"At least Buddy stops here when he gets loose," Mallory said. "And he's not roaming the streets and the neighborhood."

"Apparently, he prefers your house over his pen at the clinic."

"You may be right, but I told you before. A smaller pet would fit my lifestyle much better. I do have to admit, though, Lucas sure loves that dog. And Buddy is crazy about him."

"Speaking of Lucas," Rick said, "how's he doing? He was pretty upset with you last night."

"Things seem to be better today. He's not as talkative, but at least I'm not getting the full silent treatment. Hopefully, we'll be able to put it all behind us soon."

The sliding door opened, and Lucas poked his head inside. "Hey, Mom. Did Dr. Martinez…" When he spotted Rick, he grinned. "Oh, there you are."

Rick returned his smile. "Under the circumstances, I don't think you need to refer to me as Dr. Martinez anymore."

"Then what should I call you?" the boy asked.

Rick supposed a man probably had to earn the right to be called Dad, which he would have felt weird suggesting anyway. "How about calling me by my name— Rick."

Lucas shrugged. "Okay." Then he turned to his mother. "Can Rick stay for dinner?"

"I…" Mallory glanced at the boy, who'd remained in the doorway, blocking it so the dog couldn't come inside. Then she turned to Rick and blessed him with another one of those heart-stopping, brain-stealing smiles. "It's fine with me. We're having leftover spaghetti. I made enough to feed an army last night, so there's plenty."

"Why so much?" Rick asked.

"When I'm stressed or fidgety, I cook. So after you went home, I spent some time in the kitchen. I'd planned to freeze most of it so we can eat it on nights when I don't feel like fixing dinner. But I didn't have any suitable plastic containers yesterday. So I picked some up on my way home today."

"Are you sure you can spare an extra plate?" Rick asked.

Mallory laughed, a mesmerizing sound he hadn't heard in a long, long time, a blood-stirring lilt he'd really missed. "I can spare a *lot* of plates."

A bark sounded behind Lucas.

"I gotta go," the boy said. "Buddy's waiting for me."

When they were alone, Mallory said, "It might be best if you eat with us tonight, anyway. Brian, my . . . boyfriend, is coming for a visit on Monday. So before he does, you and I should probably get some coparenting issues settled. And it might be a good idea if we spent some time talking more to Lucas, too. He'll probably have some questions for us, and I think it's best if we addressed those sooner rather than later."

Before Brian's arrival, she undoubtedly meant.

There were a few things Rick would like to get squared away before then, too.

Of course, he'd meant what he'd said to Lucas. He wouldn't chase after a woman who belonged to another man. But if his instincts were right, Mallory hadn't forgotten what she'd once felt for Rick. And she was struggling with a few old memories, too.

That being the case, then maybe she'd reconsider her feelings for and her commitment to Brian.

Trouble was, there wasn't much time left. Monday was fast approaching.

But there was dinner this evening. Maybe, afterward, Rick would suggest that they sit on the back porch and share a glass of wine or a cup of coffee. There was a full moon tonight. A lover's moon.

And as long as she stood there looking at him like that, like she wasn't quite sure what to do with him—and with *them*—then Rick wasn't out of the running yet.

For some reason, Mallory couldn't quite bring herself to head into the kitchen and warm up the spaghetti. Instead, she continued to gaze at Rick. They seemed to be tiptoeing around the newness of their uncharted relationship, trying to put a name on it, she supposed.

Were they friends? Coparents? Former lovers?

Yes, all of that, she supposed. But there seemed to be more than that going on, too. But wasn't that the way it had always been between her and Rick?

Ever since she could remember, and maybe before that, she'd been drawn to strays, whether they were dogs or cats or kids no one wanted to sit with in the school cafeteria. So it really hadn't been any wonder she'd been attracted to Rick Martinez, the boy who'd been most likely to end up in jail.

Of course, his bad-boy reputation had made her a little uneasy, but she'd found it alluring, too. Those amazing blue eyes, that crooked grin and that sexy, James Dean swagger had sent her hormones raging.

She'd denied the sexual attraction at first, telling herself he was off-limits for a girl who was determined to attend college back east. But the feelings had grown steadily stronger, especially when he appeared to be making some major changes. And in spite of her reservations, their romance had soared.

But then it had crashed and burned, she reminded herself. And she'd been leery of getting involved with strays and rebels ever since.

"I'm going to warm up dinner and set the table," she said.

Rick nodded toward the sliding door. "Unless you need some help in the kitchen, I think I'll go out and talk to Lucas."

"Go ahead. I'll let you know when everything is ready."

He nodded, then let himself outside.

She watched him go. To be honest, she was still drawn to Rick. And that was a problem, especially if she was considering marriage to another man. But each day she spent in Brighton Valley, each time she and Rick crossed paths, it became more and more evident that she couldn't continue to plan a future with Brian until she resolved a few issues left over from the past.

So how did she go about telling Brian that he shouldn't make such a big move, at least not yet? And maybe not ever?

He was going to assume her hesitation had something to do with Rick, although that wasn't entirely true. It's not as though she'd chosen one man over the other.

Rick had a questionable past. And his family history had always been a bit worrisome to her grandparents.

It ought to worry you, too, Grandpa had often said back then.

Mallory supposed it had worried her, too. Rick's father had abandoned the family when he and his brother were young. And his uncle, who'd taken them in after his mom had died, had spent time in prison for domestic violence. His younger brother had even run away from home and had never been heard of since.

Rick, of course, had made something of his life. But would he snap? Would he ever revert back to the way in which he'd been raised?

She'd asked herself that when she'd been pregnant with Lucas, although that question didn't hold much water these days. Not when Rick had made so many changes and had done so much with his life.

How could she not be proud of him now?

No, like it or not, she was going to have to tell Brian that she needed some time to get settled into her new life. She would then suggest that he put that job transfer on hold for a while. If he decided to break up with her over it, then so be it. She'd just have to deal with that.

And if Rick…

Well, she'd just have to worry about Rick later, too.

Right now, Rick Martinez was the least of her problems. Because first she had to talk to Brian. And that would have to take place on Monday—in person and face-to-face.

Rick stood on the porch for a while, watching Lucas and Buddy play ball. Finally, he approached his son.

"Lucas, I need to ask you something. And I want an honest answer. Did you let Buddy out of his pen today?"

The boy was just about to launch the ball across the

yard, but stopped in midthrow. He turned to Rick and said, "Yes, I let him out."

Rick raked his hand through his hair. He really ought to scold the boy, especially since Buddy could have been hit by a car. But maybe Lucas hadn't meant to let him out.

"How did that happen?"

"I…" Lucas bit down on his bottom lip. "Well, I hope you don't get mad about this, but I let him out on purpose."

"Without my permission?"

"I'm sorry, Dr. Martinez. I mean Rick. But I was trying to help. And Buddy stayed right beside me. He didn't even need a leash because he likes to be with me all the time."

Rick wanted to clamp down on the kid, to tell him that he was way out of line. Maybe he should go so far as to prohibit him from coming to the clinic and playing with Buddy for a while—or at least from visiting the rescue yard. But he hated to come down too hard on him. After all, they were just getting to know each other.

Shouldn't they become friends before he started to discipline him?

"What did you mean when you said you were just trying to help?" Rick asked. "Who was in trouble this time?"

"You and my mom. Remember when Buddy got out that first day we moved here and ran into our house with muddy feet? It brought you guys back together. And I thought, if he came home with me and I let him into the house again, you would have to come and get him. And then she'd invite you to stay for dinner. And she did."

"Actually, *you* invited me. And she just said it was okay."

"Well, it worked, didn't it?" Lucas looked up at him with such a bright, hope-filled expression that it was hard to get angry at him, even though his whole goofy ploy had been stupid at best.

Nevertheless, it was crazy. And it didn't make a lick of sense. Rick clicked his tongue and slowly shook his head. "I don't get it, Lucas. I thought you were mad at your mom—and at me."

"I am mad—mostly at her. But that doesn't mean I don't love her. Or that she isn't my mom and you aren't my dad."

Rick had to give his reasoning some thought, especially since he seemed to think that he could be angry at someone yet not yell and scream or run away. Yet beyond that, he'd also been trying to see his family come together again.

Poor kid.

Buddy barked, then ran to the sliding door and barked again.

"What's the matter, boy?" Rick followed the dog to the glass slider.

When he saw Mallory walk to the front door, he realized someone must have knocked. He didn't think anything about it until Lucas said, "Uh-oh. What's *he* doing here? He's going to ruin everything."

Rick watched as Mallory welcomed a tall, fair-haired man into the house.

"Who's that?" he asked, although he had a pretty damn good idea who it was.

"It's Brian. And he's not supposed to come until Monday."

Mallory had told Rick the same thing, but apparently the guy had surprised her. It looked like the surprise was on Brian, though.

Or on Mallory.

But maybe the biggest surprise of all was on Rick. Because, as he studied the guy through the glass door, as he noted the stylish slacks and shirt, the broad shoulders, the muscular arms....

For some reason, Rick had thought that Brian was a nerd—probably because Lucas had led him to believe that. But Brian was every bit as handsome and well-built as Mallory deserved.

So if the guy wasn't into sports, as Lucas had said, how'd he get so muscular?

Well, Rick wasn't going to find out by hanging around outside with Lucas and the dog.

"Maybe we ought to go inside and get the introductions over with," Rick said.

"I don't have to. I already met him, so I'm going to just stay out here with Buddy."

Rick took another peek inside, watched as Brian brushed a kiss on Mallory's lips, grimaced as his gut twisted and his fists clenched at his sides.

Damn. Mallory was just as out of his reach now as she'd ever been.

He probably ought to forget the dinner invitation. In fact, a nice guy would slip the leash onto Buddy's collar and take him around the side gate, let himself out and walk home, with no one the wiser.

But sometimes Rick just couldn't seem to kick the rebel he'd once been.

Chapter Ten

Mallory couldn't see the color of her cheeks, but if the heat in them was any indication, they had to look as if she'd been out in the sun all day.

"I didn't expect you until Monday," she said, as she led Brian through the living room.

"Surprised?" he asked.

Shocked was more like it. And annoyed, too. "Why didn't you call?"

"Because," Brian said, "each time I did, it seemed as if you couldn't find time to talk. You were always on the run—either to a job interview or to visit or your grandfather. Or else you were picking up Lucas or dropping him off. I finally decided it was time we talked in person, and I wasn't about to wait another day."

At that point, the sliding door opened, although she ignored it and responded to Brian's complaints.

"I'm sorry you felt neglected. It's just that my schedule has been so erotic. I mean, *erratic*." Her eyes widened at the unfortunate mistake, and even though she'd tried to correct the blunder, it hadn't gone unnoticed.

"That was an interesting slip of the tongue," Brian said. "Or maybe it was Freudian."

Footsteps sounded as someone entered the house. She wasn't exactly sure who it was since her back was to the door, but there were only two people in the backyard—Rick and the boy who looked just like him.

By the way Brian was gazing over the top of her head, she suspected it hadn't been Lucas.

As if on cue, Rick entered the room, making things a lot more Freudian than interesting to Brian.

Her cheeks heated to a second-degree burn and, no doubt, provided more fodder for Brian's suspicions.

She didn't dare steal a glance at Rick, who must have heard the whole thing and was probably finding it all amusing.

Instead, she decided to play it cool and introduce the men.

"Brian," she said, "this is Rick Martinez."

"Let me guess," he said, his tone a bit testy. "You're the boy's father."

The *boy's* father?

Mallory's anger rose by the second, and she wasn't sure who ought to be the biggest target. Brian was certainly in contention for popping in unexpectedly to either surprise her or check up on her—she wasn't entirely sure which. And then there was Rick, who infuriated her for… Well, for just being Rick and for always complicating her life whether he tried to or not.

For some reason, Rick seemed to bring out the worst

in her, making her forget everything she'd ever been taught, everything she'd ever planned, everything she'd ever believed about herself.

As the clock on the mantel ticked on, things seemed to go from awkward to unbearable.

Mallory might have invited Rick to dinner, and while she couldn't very well withdraw the invitation now, it would certainly be nice if he graciously bowed out.

Again the slider opened, and this time Lucas entered the room. He glanced first at Brian, then at Rick.

"How's it going?" Brian asked him.

"Okay."

"So where are you staying?" Mallory asked, making sure that both Rick and Lucas knew that Brian wasn't going to sleep at her house. Although, for the life of her, she wasn't sure why she gave a flying leap why it mattered what Rick thought.

"In Wexler," Brian said. "The only place I could find in Brighton Valley was a two-bit motel next to a honky-tonk. What's with this town?"

Brian, too, seemed to be on edge for more reasons than one. Was he jealous? Suspicious? Angry?

A combination of all three?

Mallory felt badly about what she'd put him through, especially after all he was prepared to give up for her. She needed to reverse things or at least set them into slow motion now, but she wasn't sure how to go about doing it, especially with an audience.

Before she could come up with a feasible game plan, that crazy dog started to howl.

As if she didn't have enough to worry about.

When Rick excused himself to check on Buddy, Lucas followed him outside.

"This isn't what you think," Mallory said.

Brian crossed his arms. "What *do* I think?"

She felt as though she were sitting on some kind of hot seat, and she hadn't done anything to deserve it. "I have no idea what's going on in your mind. But you caught me completely off guard. We need to talk, but not today—not tonight. I can explain. Just give me a chance to get through this evening. And for the record, Lucas invited his father over for dinner. I can assure you that it's going to be a very early night. In the morning, I'll ask the neighbor to look after Lucas. You and I can meet somewhere for a late breakfast. Then we can talk—in private."

Brian uncrossed his arms. "I've been more than patient, Mallory."

"I know you have. You're a great guy, Brian. And I'm lucky to have you."

It's just that Mallory didn't feel very lucky right now.

And what little luck she'd had in the past seemed to have run out.

When Buddy had started howling and scratching at the glass door, Rick knew he couldn't very well let the dog continue to make a racket like that. He also knew that he and Buddy had both worn out their welcomes.

But that was just as well. To be honest, he didn't want to stick around any longer. He'd seen enough. And he was ready to go. He wouldn't have minded sticking around to see Brian simmer and stew, of course. But it nearly killed him to see Mallory suffer.

So after excusing himself, he'd gone out to the backyard, the leash in his pocket.

Lucas, who'd followed him out, said, "You're going to come back, though. Right?"

"No. After I take Buddy home, I'm going to stay there."

"Why? You're supposed to eat dinner with us tonight."

"Lucas, your mother's boyfriend is here."

"Yeah, but did you see the look on her face? She's not happy about him being here."

"She's not happy because he's upset. And if I leave, that should make him feel better—and her, too."

"Well, it won't make *me* feel better. Or you, either. Right?"

Rick didn't answer. Instead, he snapped the leash onto Buddy's collar.

Lucas reached for his forearm and held firm. "Come on, Rick. Do something."

"There's nothing I can do."

"There has to be. You used to love each other, and I think you still do. She shouldn't be going out on dates with someone else, especially when that guy wants to marry her."

Rick wanted to argue, to deny his feelings. But how could he do that when the boy was right. And when he'd promised not to lie to him?

"Lucas, we talked about this already."

"I know. But that was different. Brian is here now. And you're leaving."

Rick blew out a sigh. "No matter how you feel about Brian, your mom has to make that decision for herself."

"But I saw you guys last night. After I went to my room, I went back to tell you something. But I didn't because of the way you were looking at each other. You touched her face like you wanted to kiss her—really bad. And she wanted you to."

The boy had almost a sad desperation to his tone, and even though Rick had wanted to deny it, he couldn't bring himself to.

The truth was, he'd been pretty damn close to kissing Mallory. And she might have let him—boyfriend or not.

"If you would have kissed," Lucas added, "it wasn't going to be the kind that moms and dads give their kids. Or the kind old friends give each other. I watch TV. And I used to see my parents kiss. Those are the real kind. You know what I mean?"

Rick knew exactly what he meant. That's why, even though he'd dated quite a bit after he and Mallory had split, he'd never made any commitments to anyone else. How could he when he'd never met another woman whose kisses had touched him the way Mallory's had?

And that was the weird thing about it. She'd been a virgin when they'd met, and he'd been the experienced one. As things had heated up between them, as they'd grown more intimate, he'd known that things would be different—and special, because she was special.

Then one night, one of those "real" kisses had exploded with passion, and they'd made love in the backseat of her grandfather's car. Rick had assumed that he was going to teach Mallory something that night, but it had been the other way around.

He'd learned there was a big difference between sex and making love. And from then on, even though he'd dated and had sexual relationships, he'd never gotten serious with anyone else again because he'd never wanted to settle for anything less.

"Don't you still love her?" Lucas asked. "Even a little?"

Rick had never talked about his feelings with anyone, let alone a kid. But then again, he'd never been a father before. "Yeah, Lucas. I love her. But there's not much I can do about it."

"You can fight for her," Lucas said.

Once upon a time, Rick wouldn't have thought twice about a fight—be it physical or verbal. But those days were long behind him now.

Besides, how did a man fight for a woman he'd once believed was too good for him?

"I could help," Lucas said.

Rick smiled and ruffled his son's hair. It was nice to know he had a pint-size fight manager in his corner. "Thanks, Lucas. But as long as Brian is in town, there's nothing either of us can do."

Then Rick led Buddy to the side yard, opened the gate and walked his dog home, wishing things could be different.

And knowing that some things would never change.

Rick hadn't come back into the house last night, which had been fine with Mallory. Brian's unexpected presence had been enough drama to deal with.

She'd felt badly sending him off to the hotel soon after he'd arrived, but she'd wanted some time to sort through her thoughts and feelings.

And while she'd told Brian that she and Lucas were going to make it an early night, it hadn't turned out that way for her.

First, Lucas had followed her into the kitchen and had quizzed her about her feelings for Rick.

"Did you used to love him?" he'd asked.

She hadn't wanted to have that conversation with him, especially last night, but she'd felt compelled to respond—and truthfully. "Yes, I did love him back then."

"Do you still love him?" he'd asked.

"It's complicated," she'd said, hoping that would appease him until she had time to sort through her muddled emotions. She definitely still had feelings for him.

"Do you love Brian?" Lucas had asked.

"I care about him."

"You're not going to marry him, are you?" The boy's expression, as well as his question, held a desperate plea that reached deep into her heart.

Even if she hadn't promised to be honest with him, she didn't think she could have skated around the truth. "No, Lucas. I don't think so. I have to talk to him. I just don't know what to say—or how to say it."

His expression and his mood lightened. "It shouldn't be that hard."

Maybe not to a child. But to a woman who didn't like to hurt the people who cared about her, the people who'd been kind and supportive and loving…?

"You have no idea how tough this is going to be for me. Hopefully, I'll think of something by the time I see him tomorrow at ten."

"I could help."

At that, she'd smiled and brushed a kiss on his brow. "I'm afraid this is something I have to do for myself. But thanks for wanting to help me—that's very sweet of you. Good night, Lucas. I love you."

"Love you, too."

After Lucas had gone to bed, she'd spent hours in the kitchen, first freezing the leftover spaghetti, then baking cookies and several loaves of banana bread she would share with Alice.

When she'd finally turned in, she'd lain awake until just after two, thinking about the heartbreaks she'd suffered in the past, the dilemma she faced now and the total uncertainty of the future.

As a result, she'd slept in much later than usual and didn't wake up until her cell phone rang, jarring her to her senses.

She fumbled for it on the nightstand and said "Good morning" without checking the display.

But instead of the pleasant response she'd been expecting, she heard, "What in the hell is going on?"

Mallory pressed the cell phone closer to her ear, as if she hadn't heard Brian's words. But there was no mistaking his question or his brusque tone, and a surge of guilt shot clean through her, even though it felt undeserved and unearned.

"What are you talking about?" she asked, sitting up in bed and combing her fingers through her sleep-tangled hair.

"I sensed something was up the minute you told me you were moving to Texas. Yet, fool that I am, I believed and trusted you. But my brother was right all along."

"About what?"

"That you were never as invested in this relationship as I was."

She wanted to explain, to defend herself, but maybe he was right. When her life had turned upside down and she'd been dealt devastating blows, such as Sue's death and her grandfather's illness, she hadn't turned to Brian. She'd withdrawn from him instead, choosing to deal with them on her own. It was her way of handling problems, she supposed, because she'd done the same thing with Rick way back when.

But this wasn't the kind of conversation she wanted to have on the telephone. She'd planned to have it today, at brunch.

"And then I get that crazy email," he said.

"What email?"

"The one that was signed by you, although I suspect you weren't the one who wrote it."

"What are you talking about?" She glanced at the clock on the bureau, wondering if she'd actually awakened or if she was in the middle of some bizarre dream. "We're supposed to meet in an hour and a half. Why would I send you an email?"

"I figured that much since you addressed me as *Brain.* And I also hoped that a college graduate would use the correct form of the word *break* when telling me she didn't want to go out with me anymore."

"Oh, my gosh. Brian, I'd *never* send you an email like that. And if I wanted to break up with you, I never would have ended things that way. I would have—"

"Done it over brunch?" he asked.

She didn't answer. Had he always suspected that had been her plan, or was he only coming to that conclusion now?

Either way, after all the thought she'd given to it last night, that had been her decision. But she wasn't going to tip her hand until she saw him in person.

She took a deep breath, then slowly blew it out. "Can you please forward that email to me?"

"Yes, but I suspect you'll have a copy in your Sent Mail."

So did she. There was only one explanation, and her stomach curdled at the thought.

"If you didn't send it," Brian said, "then you must suspect the same person I do. It certainly looks like it was written by a nine-year-old."

"Yes, I think you're right. But I still I can't believe Lucas would do something like that."

"I can. He obviously wants to see you and his father back together again. And if you've been seeing Rick on a regular basis and having him over for dinner when I'm not around, then you can't blame Lucas for thinking that the two of you might reunite."

"I'm sorry, Brian. Dinner last night was just a casual thing. We were having leftovers—not a fancy meal." She didn't bother telling him that she and Lucas had ended up eating alone.

Silence filled the line for a moment, although it felt more like an aeon. Finally Brian asked, "Are we still on for brunch?"

"Yes." She and Brian needed to have a long-overdue talk.

In the meantime, so did Mallory and Lucas.

After they decided to meet at the café next to his hotel, she ended the call. Then she booted up her computer. Apparently, she shouldn't have kept the password to her email account stored. She certainly wouldn't do that again.

Once she logged on, she checked her Sent Mail folder. And sure enough, there it was.

Dear Brain.
I am sorry. We shuld brake up. Maybe you shuld stay in Boston for a year. We can talk then.
Your friend.
Mallory.

She'd been hacked. By her nine-year-old son.

Mallory knew that Lucas had never really warmed up to Brian, but she'd hoped that, with time, he would get to know him better and give him a chance.

Obviously he wanted to see her and Rick back together, which was understandable. But he'd gone too far in his matchmaking attempts.

As a precaution, she changed her password, then changed his, as well. After signing off and shutting down the computer, she went into the den, where he was playing a video game.

"I just got a call from Brian," she told him. "Turn off that game. In fact, you're going to need to disconnect the PlayStation completely. You're grounded."

"Aw, man." He turned to face her. "Why?"

"For sending an email to Brian and signing my name. For hurting his feelings and trying to destroy our friendship. I'm hurt, angry and embarrassed, Lucas. And I'm ashamed that you would do such a thing." Mallory blew out a sigh. "When were you going to tell me?"

"As soon as you woke up, but I didn't get a chance."

Mallory combed her fingers through her hair, wishing this was all a dream.

"I was only trying to help. Besides, you told me that you didn't know what to say to him."

"Yes, but it wasn't your place to speak for me. It was mine. And you went *way* too far in trying to help. For that reason, you're grounded."

"What's grounded mean?"

"It means that you're getting a time-out from the computer. You won't be able to use it unless I'm seated beside you. And even then, it will only be for homework purposes. You'll also lose your privileges for watching television and from any and all electronic devices."

"For how long?"

The rest of your life, she was tempted to blurt out. But that would have been her anger talking. So she reined it in and said, "I'm not sure yet. After I cool down, I'll give you an actual date."

Apparently his conscience must have finally kicked in because he didn't put up any more argument. Instead, he shut off the game and disconnected it from the television, just as she'd asked him to.

"Why would you do something like that?" she asked. "Don't you like Brian?"

"He's okay. It's just that I like Rick better. He loves you, and I was helping him fight for you."

Rick *loved* her? Surely Lucas was mistaken. He'd merely connected some dots that hadn't been there.

But what had he meant when he said he was helping Rick fight for her? Had Rick been working on the boy? Had he put Lucas up to hacking into her email account?

She couldn't believe Rick would encourage their son to sabotage her relationship with Brian. Of course, the two of them had had plenty of time to talk privately last night when they'd been outside with the dog.

But still, Lucas had gone beyond anything she would have ever done as a child. But then again, she didn't have a rebellious bone in her body.

His father did, though.

The more she thought about the probability of Rick's involvement, the angrier she grew. She'd been so complacent, so eager to please those around her that she'd allowed herself to be manipulated by everyone she'd ever loved. Even her nine-year-old son thought he could force her hand.

"You know," she added, "I'm also going to forbid you to visit the veterinary clinic for the time being."

"You're grounding me from my *dad?*" Lucas asked, his eyes growing wide in disbelief. "You *can't* do that."

Intellectually, she knew that she couldn't, that she shouldn't. But emotionally speaking, it certainly seemed like the right thing to do. At least, as far as she was concerned.

Because right now, Mallory needed a time out, too— from Rick Martinez.

Chapter Eleven

Ever since Clay Jenkins had called this morning, Rick hadn't been able to do much more than stare at the television screen, and it wasn't even on. He'd never been prone to dark moods, but the news he'd received—or the lack of it—had really sent him into a tailspin.

He took a sip of his morning coffee, which had gone cold, just like the only lead he'd had to Joey's whereabouts, a friend who'd said he'd dropped him off at the bus depot in Wexler the day he ran away from home.

Yet despite Clay's amazing tech skills and a thorough internet search, he hadn't been able to find any other clues. Once Joey had boarded that bus and left Brighton Valley ten years ago, he'd vanished somewhere between Houston and California.

How did a guy disappear like that?

Rick supposed Joey might have changed his name

and created a brand-new life for himself, which is what he hoped he'd done. After all, Joey had been pretty angry at Rick when he'd left town.

The other alternative—that Joey had met an untimely death—was hard to consider. In fact, the possibility had haunted him for years. What if Joey's body hadn't been found? Or, if it had, what if it hadn't been identifiable? There's no way anyone could have notified his next of kin, so he would have been buried in a potter's field with other unknown and unclaimed victims.

Several times after Clay's call, Buddy had nudged Rick's hand with a cold nose, trying to get a pat. Rick had complied, just as he was doing now.

At first he'd figured the dog was just trying to get some attention, but now he wondered if Buddy had sensed his sadness and was actually trying to cheer him up.

That being the case, Rick gave his furry friend's ears an affectionate rub. "You're a good dog, Buddy. At least, you try to be."

Buddy laid his head on Rick's knee and looked up at him with sympathetic eyes. All the poor dog wanted was to find someone who'd love and accept him, someone who'd give him the chance to return the affection.

The dog wasn't different from a lot of lonely people in need of a family—or just in need of someone to love them back.

Still, in spite of Buddy's efforts, Rick couldn't seem to kick his guilt, sadness or…

Hell, he didn't even know what it was. He supposed it was an almost overwhelming sense of loss. Joey had been the only family Rick had ever truly felt close to.

And it was looking more and more like his brother was lost to him forever.

And then there was Mallory, who'd once represented the family he'd hoped to create. He'd written her off years ago, then that hope had been rekindled when he found her again. But it looked as though she was still lost to him.

He had Lucas, though. And that in itself was enough to lift his mood.

Imagine that. Rick had a son, a boy who looked a lot like Joey. An inquisitive, creative and loyal kid who might even have a bit of a rebellious streak, similar to the one Rick once had.

It tickled the heck out of him to think that he and Mallory had created such an amazing child.

He wasn't sure what kind of a father he would be, but he'd certainly try his best not to ever let his son down. And while he might not live in the same house with Mallory and Lucas, he definitely planned to be a part of the boy's life.

A big part.

Would their relationship ever develop to the point that Lucas would want to call him Dad?

Rick knew he'd probably never hold a candle to Gary Dunlop, the man who'd adopted Lucas and who'd set the Daddy benchmark, but he was sure going to try.

Buddy gave his hand another nudge, and Rick smiled. "You and I are in the same boat. We're both strays in need of a family. But as long as we've got each other, we'll be okay."

Buddy gave a little bark, as if voicing his agreement.

"Well, enough of this," Rick said. "I'm not going

to waste any more time feeling sorry for myself this morning."

With that, he got to his feet, went into the kitchen and dumped the rest of his coffee into the sink. He'd no more than returned to the small living area when a knock sounded.

Buddy barked again, then trotted to the door.

Rick had no idea who'd be coming by his place on a Saturday morning. When he reached the door, he slipped his hand through Buddy's collar to hold him back before answering.

As he swung open the door and spotted Mallory on his porch, his heart slipped into overdrive. She was wearing a pair of faded blue jeans and a pink T-shirt. With her hair pulled back in a ponytail, she looked more like the girl he'd gone to school with rather than the professional social worker she'd become.

He would have tossed her a bright-eyed grin if she hadn't been glaring at him.

Should he invite her in? Something told him she didn't expect him to, so he held off.

"What's the matter?" he asked.

"Did you know that Lucas wanted me to break up with Brian?"

Apparently Lucas had been working on her, too. But she didn't look too happy about it. "Yes, he mentioned something about that."

Her scowl deepened to a frown, causing a deep crease to mar her brow. "Did you tell him that my relationship was my business and not his?"

Buddy lunged forward, his tail wagging, as if to welcome her. But Rick held him back. "I'm not sure if that came up. For the most part, I just listened to him."

"And encouraged him?" She crossed her arms and shifted her weight to one hip.

"I didn't discourage him, if that's what you mean. What are you getting at?"

"Sometime last night, Lucas signed into my email account and sent a Dear John letter to Brian—or rather a Dear *Brain* letter. He misspelled a few words. So, fortunately, Brian realized it hadn't actually come from me."

Rick couldn't help but chuckle at how the misspelled words had backfired, about how Lucas had gotten caught.

When Mallory's eyes widened and she gasped, his chuckles ceased.

"I can't believe you'd take something like that so lightly. Lucas hacked into my email account, Rick. He violated my trust. Getting involved in my personal relationship like he did was way out of line."

When she put it that way, Rick could see why she'd be upset. "I'm sorry, Mal. I wasn't trying to make light of the situation. It's just that the way he got caught was kind of funny."

"I need you to back me up on this. He can't interfere in my life like that."

She was right, but to be honest, Rick liked knowing that his son had chosen him over Brian.

"I can back you up," he said, "but don't you think he should be allowed to voice an opinion?"

"Yes, if he says something to me privately and respectfully. But he can't try to influence my decisions or dictate my choices."

"I agree."

Her stance seemed to soften a bit—finally. But she didn't smile, didn't unfold her arms.

Like Rick, even Buddy seemed to grow still, to lay low and gauge her mood.

"Did you punish him?" Rick asked.

"I took away the computer. He can only use it for homework—and then, only when I'm seated beside him. He's also lost the PlayStation, as well as the television."

"It looks like you have it handled, then."

"Yes, but I still need your support."

"I'm not sure what you want me to do. You punished him. And the way I see it, the punishment more than fits the crime. Why do I need to get involved at this point?"

She stiffened again. "Because I also told him he couldn't stop by the clinic for a while."

Now it was Rick's turn to take offense. What was she saying? That she'd grounded Lucas from seeing Rick, too? Not that he hadn't wanted to punish the boy for letting Buddy out the other day. To be honest, he'd actually considered restricting his visits to the clinic or the rescue yard in order to teach him a lesson, but that was different. Completely different.

"Did you hear me?" she asked. "If Lucas stops here, I want you to send him home. And to reprimand him."

Rick hadn't been called on the carpet like this since he'd been in high school. He'd bristled at it then, and he didn't like it any better now.

In spite of his feelings for Mallory, and his agreement that she did have a point, he found himself crossing his own arms. "No, Mallory, I can't go along with that."

"I'm sorry, Rick, but this is serious. I don't want Lucas to grow up to have little regard for a person's privacy. He needs to learn respect and common courtesy and…"

And all the things Rick hadn't learned growing up?

His eyes narrowed, and he shot a glare right back at her. "Apparently, you're going to have to be the disciplinarian, Mallory. You seem to know all the rules."

She shook her head and clucked her tongue. "What kind of father are you?"

Mallory couldn't have struck him any harder if she'd swung a baseball bat and hit him right between the eyes.

He wanted to object, to tell her she wasn't being fair, that she was punishing him, too. But, as she turned and walked away, as Buddy barked and fussed, Rick held onto the dog's collar, as well as his temper, and kept his mouth shut.

After all, that probably would make it easier on all of them.

He'd given up his paternal rights before, thinking it was for the best.

Maybe that had been the right decision all along.

Mallory arrived ten minutes late at the Picadilly Café in Wexler, thanks in part to her decision to stop by Rick's place before meeting Brian. But she'd been so angry with Lucas and so determined to confront Rick that nothing else had mattered.

After parking her car, she joined Brian at one of the outdoor umbrella-shaded tables in front, where he was already having a cup of coffee.

Fortunately she'd called to let him know she was running a little behind schedule.

"I'm sorry you had to wait," she said, as she took a seat across from him.

"I've gotten used to it."

In the past he would have said that it wasn't a problem, but clearly that was no longer the case. And as annoyed as she'd been with him earlier, she really couldn't blame him in the scheme of things. "That's just it, Brian. You really shouldn't have to wait on me."

"I know."

The waitress stopped by with two menus. "Can I get you some coffee?" she asked Mallory.

With as topsy-turvy as her tummy was, especially after the ugly confrontation with Rick, she was leery about eating or drinking anything. But she wanted to move things along. "I'd like some hot tea, please."

When the woman left them, Mallory glanced down at her paper placemat. She fiddled with the scalloped edge for a moment, then forced herself to face things head-on. "I want you to know that I think the world of you, Brian."

"Here it comes. The big *But*."

They both knew where this conversation was going, but that didn't mean she planned to disregard his feelings.

Brian sat back in his seat. "Let me help you out. You moved back to your hometown and decided to reconcile with your high school sweetheart."

"I'm afraid it's not that simple. Moving back here has been a real eye-opener for me in many ways, but you also mentioned something last night that really struck a chord."

"What's that?"

"You said that I withdrew from you whenever things got tough. And you were right. It was completely subconscious on my part. You offered me your shoulder to lean on, which was a gift. But I failed to use it—or to appreciate it."

"So what do you think that means?" He leaned forward, placing his elbows on the table, while he held his coffee mug with both hands. "It tells me that you're not as emotionally connected to me as you should be."

"Unfortunately, I think you're right."

Their eyes met, and the walls she'd built up between them seemed to lower, allowing them both to face the truth.

"I've been having second thoughts, too," he admitted. "My brother and I had a long talk while we were fishing at the cabin. He'd been telling me all along that I was going to get hurt if I didn't realize that you weren't all that into me. I thought about it a couple of days, then decided to come out and see for myself whether a move to Texas was really in my best interest. And I see that it isn't. You're not in love with me, Mallory. And I doubt that you ever really were."

"I wanted to be," she said. "I really did. You're a great guy."

The waitress stopped by with Mallory's tea. "Are you ready to order?"

Brian ordered a bagel and cream cheese, saying he wasn't really hungry.

"I'll have the same," Mallory said, doubting she'd be able to do more than take a couple of bites.

"So what about Rick?" Brian asked. "Are you still in love with him?"

Was she? She'd been fighting her feelings for so long that she wasn't sure what she felt for him.

"I still care about him," she admitted, "but I don't think we'll be seeing much of each other."

"Why?" Brian asked.

"Because I stopped by his place before I came here to meet you. I wanted him to take a more active role in punishing Lucas for sending that email. And I implied that he might have even encouraged the interference."

"Was he involved?"

"He said he wasn't. But we had words, and things ended badly."

Rick had never been angry at her before, but this morning he'd been furious. So there was no telling what she could expect from him.

His father had walked out on the family when Rick had been a child. And his brother had run away as a teenager and never come back.

Rick had been so opposed to the open adoption, that he'd signed over all parental rights and had pretty much washed his hands of her and Lucas. At least, it had felt that way.

No, she had a feeling that any chance she and Rick had of rekindling their romance was over. She'd pretty much made sure of that when she'd turned on her heel and walked away.

The only one who'd seemed interested in chasing after her had been Buddy, but Rick had held him back.

Rick stuck close to home all weekend, but instead of putting Buddy back in his pen during the day, he let him stay in the house or by his side. After all, how else would the dog learn to be a family pet if he wasn't allowed to be one?

In spite of Rick's concerns, it had worked out okay. The dog had stayed out of trouble. In fact, just as Lucas had said, Buddy didn't run off as long as he had someone to stick close to.

As Sunday wore on, it seemed that Rick and Buddy had formed a bond of some kind. Or maybe Rick just appreciated having someone to talk to, someone who seemed to understand—even if that someone had floppy ears, a cold nose and four legs.

By late that afternoon, Rick realized that Buddy did best when he wasn't kept in a cage. But what was he going to do with the dog when he was seeing patients—or when he started going out on calls to various local ranches?

"So who's going to look after you during the day?" he asked Buddy.

The dog gave a half bark, half whine, then trotted over to a honeysuckle plant near the gate, dug at the ground and gave it a good sniff.

Maybe they could keep Buddy in his office—or rig up some fencing to keep him in the reception area near Kara's desk.

About that time, an engine sounded. Rick looked up to see the approaching vehicle, a white, older model Toyota Corolla. When the driver, a Latino male in his late fifties, got out, Rick recognized his uncle, Ramon.

His first thought was to say, What in the hell are you doing here? But he bit it back. Instead, he said, "How's it going, *Tío?*"

"It's good, *Mijo.* Very good." Ramon reached out, and they shook hands. "Your aunt Rosa asked me to come by and talk to you. I won't stay long."

"I want you to know that I don't hold any hard feelings toward you," Rick said, although he supposed that wasn't entirely true.

"I wouldn't blame you if you did. Things were pretty bad when you and Joey lived with us. I can apologize a hundred times, but I know that's not going to take away the bad memories."

He had that right.

"I was a lousy husband," Ramon said, "especially when I drank. And I know that some guys go to prison and come out all the worse for it. But I'm not one of them. I learned a lot there—mostly that I never want to go back."

"That's good to hear," Rick said.

"I haven't had a drink in nearly a year," he added. "I've been going to AA meetings. I have a great sponsor—a good man who holds me accountable."

Ramon never had anyone notable to look up to, anyone he could count on in a pinch. Neither had Rick—until he met Hank. So he could see where those meetings and a strong support system would help.

"My old man used to drink himself into either a rage or a stupor every night," Ramon said. "And I grew up thinking that was what all men did. But I now know that's not true. I've also joined a church, and I'm learning a new way to live. I've met some good people, seen some nice families."

Rick had felt the same way when the Lazaros had invited him into their home. Maybe his uncle really had changed. Maybe he really did want a new life for himself and Rosa.

"Your aunt is willing to give me a second chance," Ramon said. "And while I don't expect you to do that, I'm on step nine in the program, and I need to make amends with the people I've hurt. I'm sorry, *Mijo*. I can't fix the past, but I promise to be a better man in the future. I hope one day you will find it in your heart to forgive me."

How could Rick not forgive him?

"Sure, *Tío*. If *Tia* Rosa can forgive you, I can, too."

When Rick opened his arms, his uncle stepped into his embrace.

"I promise you won't be sorry, Ricardo. I won't let you down. Not again."

As Ramon turned to leave, he paused when he reached the driver's door of his vehicle and looked over his shoulder. "Oh. I almost forgot. Your *tia* wanted me to invite you to dinner one night this week. She said she'd make all your favorites—chili *verde*, chicken mole.... What do you say?"

Rick tossed him a smile. "I'll give her a call later and decide on a day that works best for both of us."

Ramon broke into a contented grin, then got into his car and drove away.

As Rick watched him go, his anger, hurt and doubts began to morph into hope.

Ramon wasn't just making false promises this time. He was actually taking solid steps toward change. And for that reason, Rick was determined to offer his support—not only in his uncle's quest to stay sober but in his desire to reconcile with his aunt.

Rick, of all people, couldn't blame the man for wanting to create—or re-create—a family for himself.

In fact, that's what Lucas had tried to do. And that's why Rick hadn't been able to fault him for it—let alone punish him.

His thoughts drifted to the whole mess with Mallory, yet no matter how angry she'd gotten at him, no matter how much blame she placed on him, he wasn't going to stand by and let her take his son away from him.

She might not believe it, but he now knew it to be a rock-hard fact. A kid who'd grown up in a dysfunctional home really could kick his past and become the man and the father he'd always hoped he could be.

Rick glanced down at the dog sitting beside him. It might take some work and a little patience, but Rick was in it for the long run. "We both are. Isn't that right, Buddy?"

As if knowing just what he was agreeing to, the dog—Rick's dog—barked.

So where did Rick go for some Daddy training?

The only man Rick had ever gone to for solid advice on anything was Hank Lazaro. And who better to go to for counsel now?

Rick reached into his pocket and pulled out his cell. When he had Hank on the line, he asked, "Do you have a minute?"

"Sure. What's up?"

"I have a problem and need some fatherly advice." Rick went on to lay it all on the table, including the details that led to the blowup he and Mallory had yesterday morning. "I'm not comfortable punishing him. He hardly knows me. And I think we need to be friends first. Besides, she came down so hard on him that I thought she was unfair."

"Well, you have two issues going on there. First of all, you and Mallory need to learn how to parent together. It's hard enough for a husband and wife to do that when they've had a child since infancy and have learned to discipline as they've gone along. But you've had the job dropped into your laps. And on top of that, you two have other issues to deal with, such as your past relationship and how that's going to affect your parenting from here on out."

"You got that right."

"I'm in no position to address your relationship issues with Mallory," Hank said, "so I won't even go there. But I can talk to you about fatherhood."

Rick didn't think anyone could help him deal with the Mallory stuff. He was still trying to wrap his mind and his heart around it himself. "Let's focus on me and Lucas."

"It's nice when a father and son can be buddies," Hank said. "But you're the adult. Sometimes you can't be a nice guy. You have to set boundaries and enforce rules whether you like them or not. And a kid will actually respect you for it. They like knowing their limits. It makes them feel loved and safe."

Rick glanced down at his four-legged "buddy." Hadn't he given similar advice to the pet owners who'd talked to him about obedience training?

"I'm sorry I can't advise you on what to do with Mallory," Hank said. "What I can do is invite Lucas to come over to our house for a sleepover tonight. That would give you two a chance to talk things over in private. And maybe you can also come up with a coparenting game plan."

"Thanks for the offer. That would be great, but I don't think it will work out, especially with Brian in town. Besides, tomorrow is a school day."

"I understand. But if you ever do need a sitter, even on a weeknight, Marie and I will make sure that Lucas gets to bed early, that he eats a good breakfast and that he gets to school well before the morning bell rings."

"Thanks, Hank. I'll remember that."

After disconnecting the line, Rick stood in the middle of his yard, giving Hank's words some thought.

Like it or not, he was going to have to talk to Mallory. And he wouldn't put if off any longer. He wasn't sure whether Brian would be there or not, but either way, he was going to apologize.

He probably owed an apology to Brian, too. If the man was going to marry Mallory, they would all have to work together for Lucas's sake.

As he reached into his pocket for the keys to his pickup, Buddy whined. In the past, he'd always locked the dog back in his pen. And apparently, Buddy knew it.

But not today.

"Sundays ought to be a family day. Where's your leash?"

Chapter Twelve

As Rick started walking toward Mallory's house, his uncle's words continued to dog him all the way.

I need to make amends with the people I've hurt... I can't fix the past, but I promise to be a better man in the future. I hope one day you will find it in your heart to forgive me.

Rick had accepted his uncle's apology. So why did the man's heartfelt vow keep niggling at him?

He intended to make amends with Mallory, and he planned to apologize to Brian, as well. On top of that, he'd become a much better man than he'd started out as, and he was determined to keep improving over time.

What was missing? What hadn't he done?

He hadn't walked a block when it hit him. There was someone he'd left out of the mix, one man he'd wronged yet had neglected to face.

"This isn't going to be easy," he told Buddy as he turned the dog around and headed back home. "But we have to see someone else first."

Ten minutes later, after he and his dog had climbed into his truck and driven across town, Rick turned left on Lone Star Lane and pulled into the only senior apartment complex in town that provided independent living as well as various levels of assistance.

He found a shaded parking spot near the main entrance. For a moment, he considered rolling down the windows and leaving Buddy in the car. It was cool enough today, and he wouldn't be long. But he'd decided to honor his commitments and promises from now on, even if he'd made them to a dog.

So he snapped the leash on Buddy's collar, hoping the place was pet friendly.

After talking to the receptionist and learning that Mallory's grandfather lived in apartment 2-C, Rick and Buddy made their way outside and along the floral-lined sidewalk.

As he and Buddy walked, a couple of ladies seated on a bench in the shade commented on the "cute little pooch" as they passed by.

One man wearing a cap that boasted his WWII veteran status stopped when he saw Buddy, reached into the pocket of his navy blue windbreaker and offered the dog a piece of bacon he'd apparently saved from breakfast.

Apparently, the residents seemed happy about Buddy's visit, but at this rate, it was going to take Rick forever to make his way to the right building.

When he finally found apartment 2-C, he knocked.

A matronly brunette wearing teal-colored scrubs answered the door and smiled. "Yes?"

"I'm Rick Martinez. I came to see Reverend Dickinson. Is he able to have visitors this afternoon?"

"Yes, of course. Please come in."

Mallory's grandfather, a tall, slender man in his seventies, had been reading in a brown recliner near a large window. He glanced up from his book when he realized a guest had arrived.

Rick drew Buddy's leash close to his side. "I hope I'm not interrupting you, sir. And I'm sorry for bringing my dog. He's housebroken, but I'll only be a minute."

"No, you're not interrupting anything." Reverend Dickinson set the novel on the lamp table. "Please come in. And don't worry about the dog. I'm an animal lover. Always have been. But my late wife was allergic to pet dander."

"I'm not sure if you remember me," Rick said.

"Actually, I do." The minister pointed to the sofa. "Please. Have a seat."

Rick complied. Buddy nosed his way over to the older man's outstretched hand, his tongue hanging out as his new friend rubbed him briskly behind an ear.

"What can I do for you?" the reverend asked.

"I came to…" Rick wasn't entirely sure how to broach the subject. "Well, I came to apologize for the way things happened ten years ago. I loved Mallory back then. And I love her now. I realize that she's involved with another man, and I'll respect that. I also want you to know that I fully intend to pay child support for Lucas—and that I plan to be a father to him in every way I can."

"I appreciate that. And I'm sure Mallory does, too."

The old man leaned back in his chair, Buddy sitting patiently at his slippered feet. "I heard that you went to college and got your degree in veterinary medicine. That's quite an achievement."

Rick had expected Mallory's grandfather to point out that Rick had done it in spite of the family he'd had, but he didn't. And Rick appreciated that.

"Thank you."

"I'm sure you can understand why my wife and I worried about you and Mallory becoming so serious when you were younger. And we… Well, we hadn't realized things would work out the way they did."

"None of us did, sir."

They sat like that a moment—quiet and introspective. Rick had never been too comfortable around Mallory's grandfather, but at least now he didn't fear a fire-and-brimstone sermon or lecture.

"I finally had the pleasure of meeting the boy last week," Reverend Dickinson said. "He looks a lot like you."

"Yes, he does. And he has Mallory's sweet temperament."

Again, the silence settled around them.

"Other than Alice Reilly," the reverend said, "most people don't know that Mallory was pregnant when she went to Boston. Her grandmother and I didn't see any point in telling them. I suppose it was wrong of us to try and keep that a secret. But, at the time, it seemed like a good idea."

Rick wasn't sure what to say. He figured they'd all thought they were doing the right thing at the time, even if they'd ended up making mistakes. But he held his tongue.

"Under the circumstances, I'll be making an announcement to the congregation about Mallory adopting her biological son one Sunday in the near future." Reverend Dickinson turned to Rick. "Are you okay with that?"

"Of course I am. I'm just sorry that Mallory and I weren't married when she got pregnant. But I can't change the past. I am, however, proud to call Lucas my son. And I hope that, someday, you'll be able to forgive me and to accept me as his father."

"I'd be a pretty poor minster if I couldn't find it in my heart to forgive others, Rick. I haven't always made the right choices in my life, either—believe it or not. And sending Mallory off to Boston was probably one of my biggest mistakes. But what's done is done. We make the best decision we can at the time, then we have to deal with the consequences and move on."

Buddy, obviously seeking the same attention Mallory's grandfather had given him earlier, placed his paw on the old man's lap.

"Well, now. You certainly are a friendly boy. What's your name?" The old man stroked the dog's back as if he was waiting for Buddy to answer him.

"This is Buddy," Rick said. "He's a stray I rescued. But I've decided to adopt him."

"There's a lot to be said about the heart of a man who loves animals. Lucas is lucky to have you in his life."

"Reverend Dickinson," the nurse said as she entered the room, "it's time for your medication."

Rick politely made his exit, feeling pretty lucky himself right then.

He just hoped his luck didn't run out. Because his

next stop was Mallory's house. And he hoped she would
be as forgiving as her grandfather had been.

By Sunday night, Mallory had spent so much time
in the kitchen trying to de-stress and problem solve that
she'd baked up a storm, used up all of her plastic containers and had run out of space in her freezer.

One would think that after Brian had left town that
she'd feel a lot better—and she did. But she now realized that, until she had a heart-to-heart talk with Rick,
her life would never get back to normal.

"So what are you going to do?" Lucas asked her as he
stood in the center of the living room, his arms crossed.

It's not as though she'd been discussing her dilemma
with her son, but since she'd grounded him from the
television, as well as the video and computer games,
he didn't have a whole lot to focus on inside the house.
So he'd obviously picked up on the fact that something
was bothering her.

Still, she couldn't very well share it with him.

"I don't know what you're talking about," she said.

"You're worried about something. I can tell. And you
told me that I can't butt into your life. So I'm not. But
you better talk to someone or else you're going to have
a heart attack or something."

Mallory stopped pacing—or whatever she'd been
doing that had caused him to take note of her unusual
behavior—and blew out a sigh. "You're right, Lucas.
But I'm perfectly healthy." The last thing she needed
was for the poor child to think that another adult in his
life was dying. "I do need to talk to someone, though.
And I've put it off long enough. Would you mind taking some cookies over to Mrs. Reilly? I have a couple

of plates I'd prepared as gifts for people. They're on the kitchen counter. Choose one for her. And while you're there, would you ask her if you can hang out with her for a while?"

"Okay, but who are you going to talk to?"

"Your father. I owe him an apology."

"Cool." A bright-eyed grin broke out on his face, as if that would solve everything.

It would certainly help, but she was afraid it was going to take more than those two little words to fix the damage she'd done when she'd raced over to his house and blown up at him yesterday.

While Lucas went to the kitchen for the cookies, Mallory searched for her purse and the car keys, although she probably ought to walk to Rick's place. It wasn't very far.

They returned to the living room at the same time. She waited for Lucas to open the door, intending to follow him out, but he paused at the threshold and let out a whoop.

He turned to her and smiled. "It looks like you don't have to go anywhere, Mom."

Mallory peered over the top of his head and spotted Rick coming up the sidewalk, holding Buddy's leash, the dog trotting along beside him.

The boy dashed outside to greet them. Rick tousled his hair, and the dog let out a happy yip.

Lucas and Buddy were definitely glad to see each other. She wished she could say the same for her and Rick, because when their eyes met, they gazed at each other in awkward silence.

Had he come to talk to her? She certainly hoped that

was the case. Her apology was going to be a lot easier to make if she knew it would be well received.

"Since you don't have to go to his house, can I stay here and hang out with you guys?" Lucas asked.

"No," Mallory said. "Your father and I have a few things to discuss, so please take those cookies to Mrs. Reilly, like I asked you to."

"Okay. But what if I take her the cookies, then come back and play with Buddy in the backyard?"

"I suppose that would be okay," she said.

After Lucas dashed off, Mallory invited Rick inside.

He halted at the entrance, though. "If Brian is here, and you'd rather I came back at another time, I'll do that. I don't want to cause any problems. But then again, I'd like to talk to him, too."

"Brian flew back to Boston yesterday."

"To pack?"

"No, to unpack. We broke up. He's not going to move to Brighton Valley, after all."

Mallory stepped aside, as Rick and the dog entered the living room.

"I hope you're still not trying to encourage me to adopt Buddy," she said in a lighthearted tone, hoping to break the ice and to ease some of the awkwardness.

"Not anymore. Buddy has a home with me now, which is why he's with me. I plan to train him to be a better behaved dog, but I can't do that when he's in his pen. And that's what I came to talk to you about."

"About training Buddy?"

"No, about being a better father. I want to spend more time with Lucas for the same reason. I can't very well teach him right from wrong if I'm not with him."

"I'd like that, Rick—in spite of what I said yesterday.

And believe it or not, I was just heading over to your place now. I wanted to apologize for blowing up like I did. I was upset, and I said things I'm sorry for, things I didn't mean. I hope you'll forgive me."

He studied her for a moment, and as he did, she gestured to the purse hanging from her shoulder, showing him that she had, indeed, been about to leave the house.

A slow smile stretched across his face, lighting his eyes, touching her heart. "I could never stay angry at you, Mal."

Relief shot through her, lifting her spirits higher than they'd been all day. All week. All… Well, higher than they'd been in years. "I'm glad to hear that, Rick. Because it will be nice to have you come around more often. Lucas loves you."

His smile faded, and his expression grew serious. "What about you, Mal? Do you think you could ever love me again?"

Did she dare admit it?

"Maybe," she said.

"Well, that's a start. And a good one. Because even though I did my best to forget you and move on with my life, you were the one thing I could never put behind me. At times I tried to convince myself that you deserved better, but that's not true. You might find someone you'd rather marry, but you'll never find someone who loves you more than I do."

Tears welled in her eyes, and a lump formed in her throat. She wasn't sure she could voice a response, even if she tried.

He reached out and cupped her face. Using his thumbs, he brushed the tears from her cheeks. So sweet, so tender. Just like he'd done when they'd been kids.

"I wasn't being honest with you when I said maybe, Rick." She sniffled and tried to smile. "I actually do love you. And I never stopped."

"I can hardly believe this is happening," he said. "I came to tell you that I wanted to be a part of our son's life, never thinking, never daring to hope, that I might become a part of yours, too."

She laughed through her tears. "And I'd just hoped that you'd be able to forgive me. But Marie Lazaro said something to me the day I met her. I didn't believe her at the time, but now I realize she was right."

"What did she say?"

"When we open our hearts to love and forgiveness, things have a way of working out just the way they're supposed to."

"Then our time is now. Let's be the family we were always meant to be."

"I'd like that," Mallory said. "I realize that it could take some time, though. After ten years, we'll probably have to get to know each other all over again."

"I don't think we'll need to do that." Rick stroked her hair. As he gazed into her eyes, her heart soared with more hope than she'd ever had before. "Some things have changed, Mal, but the important things haven't. As far as I'm concerned, we've waited long enough. I'm ready to get a marriage license first thing tomorrow morning. But if you'd rather wait, I'm willing to do that, too."

"As wild and crazy as this may sound, I don't want to wait, either."

"I hoped you'd say that."

As Rick lowered his mouth to hers, Mallory wrapped her arms around his neck and drew him close, relishing his musky scent and the feel of his embrace. She'd waited an eternity to kiss him again, to touch him, to taste him.

The moment their lips touched, the years rolled back and all the heartache disappeared as if it had never happened. As the kiss deepened, as she pressed into him, her body naturally wanting to become one with him again, she didn't think she'd ever let go.

That is, until a cheer erupted from the doorway. "Whoo-hoo! You did it!"

As they released each other and turned to face their happy son, Lucas asked, "Does this mean we get to be a family?"

"Yes," Rick said. "But just so you know, I'm also going to be a real father from now on, and not just your friend."

"I'm cool with that." Lucas glanced at Mallory, then at Rick, and back to Mallory. "So does that mean we get to live together?"

"We'll have to get married first," she said.

"So when will you do that?"

"Like I told your mom, as far as I'm concerned, ten years is long enough for me. I'm ready to tie the knot as soon as the state of Texas will allow it."

"How soon is that?" Lucas asked.

Touched by the boy's enthusiasm, Mallory smiled. "Three days after we file for the license. And your father suggested that we do that tomorrow."

"You don't want to wait longer than that, do you?" Lucas looked at her with such hope-filled eyes that it would have been tough to put it off, even if she'd wanted to.

"It's up to your mom," Rick said. "But she'll probably want to talk to your great-grandfather about it."

"Does he have to give us permission or something?" Lucas asked.

"No," Mallory said, "that's not his decision. I'll tell him what we're going to do, though."

"I'd like to officially ask for your hand in marriage," Rick said.

"You would?" She cocked her head to the side. "Do you want me to talk to him first?"

"You don't need to. I've already laid the groundwork. Buddy and I stopped by to see him before we came here. In fact, he'll probably want to perform the ceremony."

"Whoo-hoo!" Lucas shouted again. "So do I get to wear a suit and be in the wedding?"

"We wouldn't have it any other way. But three days won't give us time to plan anything elaborate. So it's going to be very small and simple."

"I'm cool with that," Lucas said as he stepped forward and embraced them both.

Mallory slipped her arms around the man and the boy she loved more than anything in the world, her heart bursting with joy. As long as they could be the family they were meant to be, she was cool with that, too.

"You know," Rick said. "I just remembered something, Lucas. Earlier today, Hank Lazaro asked if you'd like to come to his house for a sleepover tonight. It's up to your mom, of course. But I can guarantee you'll have a lot of fun."

"But if you and Buddy are going to stay," Lucas said, "I'd rather hang out here."

"It might be best if your mom and I talked over the wedding details first. Then we can share them with you in the morning. We could stop by Hank's house and have breakfast with you before school. In fact, I'll even bring donuts."

Lucas looked at Mallory. "Is that okay with you?"

"Absolutely, as long as the Lazaros don't mind."

"What about Buddy?" Lucas asked. "Can he go with me?"

Rick laughed. "I don't see why not. Hank and Marie are animal lovers."

When Lucas went upstairs to pack, Mallory turned to Rick and lowered her voice. "Did you really plan to talk to me about the wedding this evening?"

Rick's eyes lit up, and his lips quirked into a boyish grin. "We certainly can. But to be honest, I thought it might be nice to start off with a honeymoon—unless you'd rather wait for the real one."

"I think we've waited long enough."

He brushed a kiss across her lips. "Then hold that thought. I'll be right back."

And she'd be ready and waiting.

When Rick returned to Mallory's house, she met him at the door with a shy smile. Her hair hung soft and loose about her shoulders. She wore a white cotton nightgown, the neckline somewhat conservative, the fabric sheer enough to see her bare silhouette.

She stepped aside to let him in, and as she did he caught the scent of milled soap and peach-scented lotion.

Once he was inside, she locked the door to give them privacy.

"Welcome home," she said.

Home. Mallory. He could hardly wrap his heart and mind around it all.

She'd lit candles throughout the living room. And in the background, music played softly, adding to the romantic ambiance she'd created.

But nothing set his heart on fire like Mallory did. Just looking at her, knowing that she loved him, that she wanted to marry him, set his hormones racing. He could have stood there indefinitely, taking her in, but she had something more pressing in mind, because she reached for his hand.

He let her lead him upstairs to her bedroom, where she'd lit more candles, and to the queen-size bed, with fluffy white pillows that matched a goose down comforter.

Rick knew he ought to go slow, to savor the moment, but he'd waited too long for this. He pulled her into his arms, felt her body meld to his, so soft, so right. After all these years, they still fit together perfectly.

As he drew her lips to his, as they kissed, they stroked and caressed each other, staking their claims as they had the very first time they'd made love. Yet in some ways, it was even better now.

Rick slid his hand up Mallory's waist, bringing the fabric of her gown with it, as he cupped her breast. His thumb skimmed her nipple, and her breath caught. She whimpered into his mouth, and a surge of desire shot through him. He'd never loved another woman like her, never wanted another like this.

He pulled her hips forward, against his arousal, letting her know how badly he wanted her, how badly he'd missed her. He tugged at her gown, then helped as she lifted it over her head. Once it was off, she dropped it to the floor.

She stood before him, naked and lovely. His Mallory.

Her body, long and lithe, was all that he'd remembered and more. She was finally his, not just for tonight, but forever.

When he removed his shirt, he dropped it next to her gown, baring himself to her. She skimmed her nails across his chest, sending a rush of heat through his blood.

He bent and took a nipple in his mouth, and she gasped in pleasure. Then he lifted her in his arms and placed her on top of the bed, her hair splayed upon the white pillow, her body upon the comforter.

He wanted more than anything to feel her bare skin against his, but he paused for a beat, drinking in the sight of her. "You're amazing, Mallory."

A slow smile stretched across her lips. "So are you."

"I should take my time…"

"Don't. We have all night. And then we have the rest of our lives."

She was right.

He joined her on the bed and loved her with his hands, with his lips, until they were both wild with need. And then he entered her, slowly at first, enjoying the amazing feeling of being inside her again. As her body responded to his, their small corner of the world spun faster and faster until they reached a peak so high he thought they might actually touch the stars.

Finally, when she cried out with her release, they both let go in a climax that rivaled any fireworks display he'd ever seen.

Then they laid together, breaths ragged, hearts pounding. He held her close, unwilling to let her go.

"We might have been young before," he said, "but what we felt for each other was the real deal. We just couldn't make the commitment we needed to at that time. But I'm making it now, Mallory. From this day forward, I vow to love you for better or worse, in sickness and in health and for as long as we both shall live. Do you promise the same thing?"

"I do." Her eyes shone as bright as any bride's who'd worn white and stood at an altar. "Now and forever."

* * * * *

Don't miss Clay Jenkins's story,
the next book in
USA TODAY *bestselling author Judy Duarte's*
new miniseries,
RETURN TO BRIGHTON VALLEY.
Coming soon!

Available March 20, 2014

#2323 A HOUSE FULL OF FORTUNES!
The Fortunes of Texas: Welcome to Horseback Hollow
by Judy Duarte

Toby Fortune Jones knows his purpose in life. He's a cowboy and foster dad to three adorable kids. But Angie Edwards is still drifting...until she meets Toby. Suddenly, Angie gets swept up into a life she's always dreamed of...but is she ready, willing and able to make a family with the fetching Fortune?

#2324 MORE THAN SHE EXPECTED
Jersey Boys • by Karen Templeton

Tyler Noble's happily-ever-after involves nothing more than his salvage business and his rescue dog. When pregnant beauty Laurel Kent moves in next door, however, troubled Tyler finds his outlook on life slowly changing. Can "Mr. Right Now" leave his past behind to create a forever family with Laurel?

#2325 A CAMDEN FAMILY WEDDING
The Camdens of Colorado • by Victoria Pade

Dane Camden is only interested in working on his grandmother's happily-ever-after...until he meets Vonni Hunter. Eager to settle down—but not with bachelor Dane—Vonni's hesitant about taking a job planning the Camden matriarch's nuptials. But she can't deny her attraction to the hunky Camden as she realizes domestic bliss might just be closer than she thinks.

#2326 ONE NIGHT WITH THE BOSS
The Bachelors of Blackwater Lake • by Teresa Southwick

Olivia Lawson wants her boss, Brady O'Keefe, more than any raise. Brady's seemingly oblivious to her feelings, so Olivia decides to move away and start a new life. When the boss demands a reason for her departure, Olivia invents a fake boyfriend. But Brady's not buying her fib—or the sudden turn of events that might take his gorgeous assistant away forever....

#2327 CELEBRATION'S BABY
Celebrations, Inc. • by Nancy Robards Thompson

When a one-night affair leaves journalist Bia Anderson pregnant, her best friend, Aiden Woods, steps up as her child's "father"—and her fiancé. Little does Bia know, though, that Aiden's been in love with her for years, but has never acted on it. As they bond over her unborn baby, a friendship turns into the love of a lifetime.

#2328 RECIPE FOR ROMANCE • by Olivia Miles

Baker Emily Porter is shocked when her long-lost love, Scott Collins, comes back to town. Scott's got an unwelcome secret—and it's not just that he's still madly in love with Emily. Tension rises as sparks fly between the ex-lovers, but will long-buried lies destroy their relationship?

YOU CAN FIND MORE INFORMATION ON UPCOMING HARLEQUIN® TITLES, FREE EXCERPTS AND MORE AT WWW.HARLEQUIN.COM.

HSECNM0314

***

"If you didn't meet him on vacation, it must have been a trip
for work," said Brady.

"Remind me not to try and put anything over on you."

Sarcasm was one of his favorite things about her. "So, was it
in Austin? Seattle? Atlanta?"

"I definitely went to those cities. You should know. We were
there together."

She was right about that, but when business hours were
over they'd gone their separate ways. If Olivia had met men,
she'd never said anything to him. Until now.

As crazy as he knew it was, he wanted to know everything.
"Do you have a job lined up in Leonard's neck of the woods?"

"I have an offer."

"I'd be happy to give you a glowing recommendation."

She stood and walked to the doorway of his office. "Any
other questions?"

Why are you leaving me?

Brady didn't say that out loud, even though the idea of it

had preoccupied him way too much since she'd dropped her bombshell. Besides his mother, sister and niece, he had no personal attachments—yet somehow he'd become attached to Olivia. He wouldn't be making that mistake with his next assistant.

She looked over her shoulder on the way out the door. "I'll be lining up more candidates to interview. And if you know what's good for you, you'll approach this process more seriously than you just did."

"I conducted those interviews very seriously."

She ignored that. "You need to ask yourself what's wrong with the two women you saw today."

"I don't need to ask myself anything. I already know what's wrong."

"Care to share?" She put a hand on her hip.

"Neither of them is you."

***

Enjoy this sneak peek from Teresa Southwick's
ONE NIGHT WITH THE BOSS,
the latest installment in her
Harlequin® Special Edition miniseries
THE BACHELORS OF BLACKWATER LAKE,
on sale in April 2014!

⬥ HARLEQUIN®

SPECIAL EDITION

Life, Love and Family

Don't miss the second edition of the
JERSEY BOYS duet by reader-favorite author
Karen Templeton!

Tyler Noble's happily-ever-after involves nothing
more than his salvage business and his rescue dog.
When pregnant beauty Laurel Kent moves in next
door, however, troubled Tyler finds his outlook on
life slowly changing. Can "Mr. Right Now" leave his
past behind to create a forever family with Laurel?

*Look for MORE THAN SHE EXPECTED next month
from Harlequin® Special Edition®,
wherever books and ebooks are sold!*

HSE65806

SPECIAL EDITION

Life, Love and Family

Coming next month from
USA TODAY bestselling author
Victoria Pade

A CAMDEN FAMILY WEDDING

Dane Camden's only interested in working on his grandmother's happily-ever-after…until he meets Vonni Hunter. Eager to settle down—but not with bachelor Dane—Vonni's hesitant about taking a job planning the Camden matriarch's nuptials. But she can't deny her attraction to the hunky Camden as she realizes domestic bliss might just be closer than she thinks.

Look for the latest in
THE CAMDENS OF COLORADO *miniseries*
next month from Harlequin® Special Edition®
wherever books and ebooks are sold!